# EMBRACE TOMORROW WITH PASSION

## Jeremy Lowley

**Embrace Tomorrow with Passion**

Published by Felix Publishing
info.felixpublishing@gmail.com

Author and cover artwork Jeremy Lowley

ISBN: 978-1-925662-64-1   print
ISBN: 978-1-925662-65-8   digital
Other works by the author:
Please…Don't Explain
Hold Your Brother
The Honourable Lie
In the Shadow of the Truth and Other Short Stories
In the Shadow of the Truth
 Plays:
The Lady in Suite 57
Two for the Price of One
49 Not Out

Contact author: lowley.jeremy@gmail.com  .

Registration: Thorpe-Bowker, Level 1 607 St Kilda Rd, Melbourne, Victoria 3000 Australia bowkerlink@thorpe.com.au



FELIX
PUBLISHING

# EMBRACE TOMORROW WITH PASSION

## Jeremy Lowley

*An Historical Novel of Pre- Victorian England*

PART ONE

CHAPTER ONE

Gillian Hadley had lived in the glorious, bucolic Village of Chipping Norton literally all her life. She once jokingly said 'I was born here and by golly I'll die here'.   Of course, whenever anyone says that, they don't actually mean it, Well, not for at least another fifty years. So be it.  Gillian's husband Allan had been a farmer before the awful accident that changed his life forever.

Chipping Norton was a tiny village in the Cotswolds, slap bang in middle of, what was, at that time Merry Old England. The village habitat boasted of having two churches, three shops and one, very well used public house, more of that later!

The year was eighteen eleven well before the, reasonably glorious, reign of Queen Victoria. Things were about to change, most certainly in the life of Mr and Mrs Hadley. Gillian Hadley found herself delightedly, and gloriously pregnant. She already had one son Michael, Now approaching his eighth birthday. Mrs Hadley didn't have to visit the local doctor to be told that she was with child, she was a hard-working woman of the soil, and she knew perfectly well that her body was changing, and she knew why!!!

She only told Allan because he had asked her if she was 'putting on a little puddin?' Gillian sighed, then smiled at her beloved husband and, at last, told him that their eldest son – Michael was going to have a brother. How on earth did she know that? Women know these things!

Allan stared at Gillian and said pretty much what he always said, 'Ah, well that's alright then'. But he grinned as he took his younger brother Harold down to the Belle Inn, for a couple or three beers. 'Celebration you see', he guffawed.

Gillian smiled at them and very simply got on with her chores.  Her lifestyle had virtually never changed, not that she wanted it too.  She was a contented woman who insisted on doing her work

As she always had done. She could think of no real reason to alter her way of life just because she was pregnant, so, she insisted on working right up to the time she was to go into labour.

Everything was going so well, until the last two weeks!  Gillian woke up and knew instinctively that something was wrong. Her body usually did what she expected it to do, so she waited, and waited.

It was about five o'clock in the morning when she aroused Allan by shaking him, to no avail.  Then she shook, and shouted to him.  That did the trick, very well indeed. Allan immediately started to get out of bed, armed with the assurance of most farmers, that it was time to get up and get on with it! He looked at his wife and saw, in the very earliest of rays of sunrise, that Gillian had a strained expression on her face. She very quietly mouthed, 'Get the midwife''.

Allan dressed as quickly as he could. He smiled reassuringly and said, 'I'll bring her, don't you worry my little love'.    He ran as quickly as his damaged leg would take him, and arrived at the midwife's house by five forty-five.    Having awoken the midwife by knocking loudly on the door.    He abjectly apologised for the early hour, as the door quietly opened.

He started to speak again.    The midwife stopped him by saying, well, more like growling really, 'The little buggers always arrive at some ungodly hour'.    However, she got all her things together and they set of back to Allan's house. She never spoke a single word as they marched along, eventually arriving at the farm house.    They rushed upstairs, into the main bedroom and were confronted by Gillian lying on the bed panting and sweating, when they pulled the bed sheets back, they saw an enormous amount of blood with Gillian whispering, ' I think the little lambs just about here'.

'Go and put the kettle on. We'll need plenty of hot water.' The midwife took over the proceedings, and as usual, bullied the nervous father out of the room, Allan, a fine but simple man. Never, for one second, questioned why they needed that amount of water. However, hot water they wanted, hot water they shall have.

Young  Michael had woken up by then, and hc watched as his Father stoked the stove into life, and, more importantly, into useful heat. Allan seemed to be constantly taking up more and more water.  The unwritten rule is very simple, don't ask, just do it.  It was Michael's job to go to the well and replenish the water supply.

At last, by seven forty-five in the morning they first heard the sounds of a new member of the Universe squeezing into the rarefied air.

'Welcome Sebastian Rufus Hadley.' He made his entrance into the world by hitting a top C that any opera singer would nod approvingly at.

They all rushed upstairs to find that the very capable midwife had cleaned the baby and placed

it at his mother's breast.   He suckled easily and
hungrily, until both the feature players fell asleep
in the sure knowledge that they had done a good
thing.

# CHAPTER TWO

Schools are not for learning, but learning how to learn!

Sebastian led a very blessed, innocent life, but it was not without the pains of growing up in a small rural village, but then, whose is?

 When he was just four years old his father caught a bout of influenza which quickly turned out to be pneumonia, and then transmuted into double pneumonia. He lived for just six weeks after he caught the damned disease. Gillian did everything that could be done. She sat with him, and sang and cooed over him, for the last hours of his life.  He died with his devoted wife stroking his head.

Gillian watched her husband, as he silently slipped away to... Well, no one really knows where?

After the funeral Gillian did what so many country wives and mothers did in those circumstances.  She just carried on…

She now had two sons to look after. Sebastian and twelve-year-old Michael. After a short while it became obvious that she simply couldn't manage on her own.

It's important to understand, that this was a time in which people didn't have round table discussions, at least not in her family. So it was jointly decided that Allan's younger brother Harold, should move in with them and become the man of the house.

Harold turned out to be, the most splendid, if slightly wayward, brother in- law to Gillian. He not only helped to run the farm but took over the responsibility of the boys' development.

He very quickly realised that there was a natural innocence about Sebastian, however, elder brother Michael, did not share the guileless innocence of his young brother, but exhibited the slightly devious, but natural charm and brouhaha that life had dealt him. But there was a harsh side to his nature which was destined to get him into trouble, and it did!

As he grew older, the devious side of Michael's character unfolded and grew into dominance. During his teenage years he became impossible to handle.  He became a loner by choice and seemed to lose his charm, and never even bothered to make friends.  His Mother tried everything she could think of, but realised that Michael literally couldn't care less about anyone other than himself. He was a wild boy who seemed hell-bent on self-destruction.

 Harold did all that he could think of to guide him…. But at the querulous age off seventeen, Michael's robust nature stopped him from listening to any words of advice, however blatantly obvious they were.  His journey was to prove hard, and at times, downright miserable…

His story will unfold!

There was only one school in Chipping Norton; it was named, somewhat creatively, Chipping Norton School, so, without too much ado ... It was the one that all children attended, right up until the age of thirteen!

Most country boys left school at thirteen or fourteen. They believed that, by that exalted age, they had learned everything in life that was important.  So, going to work was far more valuable, and a damn site more interesting than boring old history! Guy Fawkes was a reason to celebrate the fifth of November, that was all there was to it!

Like all the other county boys Sebastian understood that he had to earn money to pay his way, and even at the tender age of eight years, he began to realise that work was the very essence of survival.  So it was, that many people influenced his development into the man he became.

In particular his Uncle Harold, a fine, fine man, well, a goodish man.... The expression, goodish, will be explained a little later on. Harold became his teacher, his surrogate father, and his friend. He was a man who always told the truth as he saw it.  Harold was his first guide, and a damn fine one at that!

Sebastian was born into the tiny farm house he shared with his family. The cottage was just outside the village boundary and was bordered by the river that flowed past the hamlet. Sebastian's ancestors certainly knew what they were doing when they chose that as the place to start their country life, all those generations ago.

So, they weren't newcomers. Their sometimes-endearing neighbours had ceased referring to them as newies. But the old folk, well, they still weren't quite sure. That took at least five generations!

Chipping Norton, being a very small rural village, made it extremely easy for everyone to know everyone else's business, private or otherwise. It didn't matter. That was the way it was in Merry Old England. For instance, they all knew who was married, and to whom. Of course they did! And, equally naturally, who wasn't.

So, without any attempt at reasonable explanation, all the good people of the village smilingly looked the other way. When hanky-panky reared its head. But 'twas frequently whispered about in dark corners. So, in simple terms, Chipping Norton was, in fact, a very typical English village! No better or worse than most of the others.

The Hamlet was very sensibly, nestled in one of the most beautiful, lush, parts of England. The natural open woodlands produced an enormous range of the finest timber in the West of England. Or, for that matter, in all of Europe. Possibly the world!

Sebastian had always loved the surrounding forest, and, from an early age, he grasped the beauty and power of the local woodlands. He knew instinctively that trees, and hence timber, would be his life's work, indeed his passion. From early development, he was taught, by his uncle, which were the types of trees that had taken many hundreds of years to grow into the tough resilient timber that would build houses, make furniture, create bridges, build carriages; but naturally, and, most importantly of all, although being a long way from the ocean the sort of timber that was ideal for ship building.  It was one of the great powers that England still prided itself in. Just ask any Englishman!

His Uncle Harold, who had been taught by his father, that is, Sebastian's grandfather. Of course, through frequent and, sometimes painful, trial and error and sheer bloody-mindedness, became one of the finest carpenters and cabinet makers in the south of England.  A reputation he unashamedly accepted!

It always seemed so natural for Harold to unbegrudgingly pass his love, and  knowledge on to his young apprentice, his nephew.  Harold was in fact, a rather easy-going man in many ways, and a charmer in all ways. He loved, pretty women, fast horses and slowly matured whisky….in that exact order.

Unfortunately, the good uncle understood virtually nothing about the practicalities of life. Therefore, he easily succumbed to the weak, but pleasant beguilings that sometimes got pushed towards him.

That's if you're lucky! In actual fact, Harold happily ushered them in with gay abandon. Well of course he did!! You see, Harold was a drinker, not of the good waters of life, but the ones that slowly but surely turn into whisky,  brandy,  gin or rum, or   anything for that matter.  It didn't seem to worry  Harold, only his liver, and no man listens to his liver when there's grog on the table.

But what Harold didn't know about timber and carpentry, simply wasn't worth knowing! He explained that most timber must be kept dry and upright during the conditioning process so that the wood fibres could slowly strengthen, and preserve themselves, without warping or splitting. Some timber could be sliced to the thickness required so that controlled bending could be achieved.  All shipbuilders knew about that absolutely vital process,

Almost instinctively Sebastian got it. He massively admired the look and feel of the wood, and of course loved the very distinctive smell of newly stacked hewn timber.

Sebastian had all the natural inquisitiveness that brought about most of the really useful intelligence that would serve him so well, all his life.

Harold went to a lot of trouble to explain the value of having the right tools, and how to look after them. A blunt saw, or a set of rough chisels were a liability and a danger to the user. Especially if they weren't sharpened and oiled properly. Sebastian was a careful learner!!

# CHAPTER THREE

There's nothing better, than a good long walk.

Very few people owned a horse and cart which was not used, primarily for work. Only the really wealthy land owners, and social elite allowed themselves the privilege of trotting around like they owned the place. Which they probably did. Ah well! Naturally, that included showing off their Sunday best. On Sunday, naturally.

Horses were the backbone of farming life, and the horse was very simply the only means of power available to the hard-working farmer. It was widely considered that a farm couldn't thrive without the use of a horse, especially at harvest time. There were some people, not too many in Chipping Norton, who owned horses, and allowed them to gallop across perfectly innocent fields, chasing equally innocent, and, usually very clever foxes.

Folk in the village thought that those scallywags were. 'Cracking on, a bit swanky there boyo.'

Sebastian was not in the slightest bit jealous of the behorsed and carted folk!  But like most young people he secretly thought, well, maybe one day.

Actually, Sebastian enjoyed walking, so hiking long distances was never a problem. Simply a good stroll. He had actually been to the thriving township of Stratford- on- Avon, twice. Yes twice.  He saw himself as a much-travelled man. Obviously, he walked all the way there, twenty-two miles. It took him nearly three days. He could easily have made better time but he was curious about his environs, and there was so much to see on the way. Sebastian was spellbound by  the enormous buildings as he passed them by. Even the roads were vastly different from the lanes he knew so well, in and around Chipping Norton. When he eventually arrived at Stratford. Sebastian was stunned at the new buildings. Some of them were three stories high, of course the old ones were pretty interesting too. But to his young eyes, new is always better.  Well of course it is!

And the way the river Avon meandered through town, really excellent, thought he!  Sebastian could see all the boats and barges moored along the river's bank. Most of them there to make a living by trading the latest goods, and sometimes sly grog! He spent two days in the city. Luckily, he found a dry spot to sleep in. and he did some chores for the green grocer to cover his food. Life was, in fact very good.

Stratford was the first really big city Sebastian had ever seen.  Apparently five thousand people lived there. Just imagine how any city could be that enormous!

On his journey back to his home town, he was lucky enough to meet a travelling salesman named Damien Irving, who was pottering his way through life, with his family and two dogs named Fred dog and Scunge. The dogs were alright, just, after you got to know them. Mr Irving told Sebastian that his horse and cart was his family's home and his business, they lived their whole life in it. Mr Irving very kindly offered him a lift back to his village, Chipping Norton of course.

Naturally he accepted, not because he was tired or lazy, but Mr. Irving filled him with the most exciting and wonderful tales of all the different places he'd been to, but more importantly, of course, the people he met as he bartered his goods up and down the country. He had actually been to London and, would you believe it, Brighton, yes, Brighton.

He had bought and sold goods, in and around, Hove. Mainly beautifully woven materials destined  to enhance the Prince of Wales' Palace, which was so very regal and ornate.  It was designed in an enormous Asian pavilion style. Quite wondrous really, if you like that sort of thing. It was obvious from Mr Irving's comments that, he wasn't entirely sure. Still, business is business!

Mr Irvine was interested in all the new inventions. Stainless Steel was the latest innovation to the market.  Mr Irvine, who hadn't actually seen the metal, but had heard all about it.  He told Sebastian that he was amazed and couldn't understand how they could make steel that didn't rust or tarnish. Just think. Ordinary steel, with the right amounts of alloys and nickel mixed with the carbon. Amazing!

He repeated himself, as though saying twice would make it all come true, and more quickly. 'Steel that doesn't go rusty.' He very wisely said that he considered it to have a pretty darn good future if it was true. But of course, only in the building industries! He couldn't imagine what else it could be used for!! Marvellous time to be living in.  Everything new and exciting.  What will they think of next? How could anything possibly go wrong?

Gillian missed her husband Allan a great deal, and, as she became somewhat older, she actually felt the pain of losing him more and more.  She yearned for his silly sense of humour—his simple goodness and his stolidity. He was a man to trust and love. Not that Harold wasn't a splendid brother-in law and, she knew that she couldn't have survived without him. But there was only one man in her life. That's all there is to it. Sebastian never really knew his father, but between his mother and Uncle Harold, Sebastian knew that he was surrounded by people who loved and cared for him, and, for the time being, that was enough.

Of the more practical things that happened to Sebastian was the inheritance of his father's set of tools. All handmade, of course, and consisting of saws and various profiled planers, and a beautiful set of chisels. Sebastian was very proud of them and looked after them as though his father was watching over him.

Sebastian's brother Michael had left home a number of years ago. Literally no one in the village had the faintest idea where he had disappeared to. The family didn't really know if he was alive or dead. They had all craved to do whatever they could for him, but to no avail. Gillian Hadley tried everything she could think of to guide the boy. Nothing had any effect on him, however as a mother, deep down, she agonised that she had failed him. She didn't know what anyone could have done, but there was always that nagging doubt. It was a hard lesson to accept!

CHAPTER FOUR

Work is a life time hobby, just allow it to be!

Once Sebastian had reached the age of eighteen years, he decided to do the best he could to provide comfort for his aging mother. He was going to be a timberman, and everything that went with it.  It was obvious really. An abundant amount of the finest timber on his very doorstep. He concluded, with his Uncle's advice that traditional carpentry was the only way to manufacture furniture of the quality that he demanded of himself.  Nothing less would do!

Sebastian agreed wholeheartedly with Harold's basic philosophy, the tongue and groove joint, was the right way to conjoin timber together, and coupled with suitable, natural glue, ensuring that they stayed together for hundreds of years. Maybe even longer.... Sebastian simply would not have nails or screws in the workshop.

All his work would be manufactured to the stringent levels of yesteryear! He somehow understood, early on in his training, that he, more than anyone else, had to believe in the quality of his work including the selection of the right timber for the furniture. There would be times in his life when his overconfidence would be viewed as infuriating. The only thing one can do in those circumstances is nod your head knowingly, and walk away as quickly as possible. Preferably with a character driven smile on your face, if you can squeeze it out!

On a more practical level, and at a young age, he quickly realised that you can ask more for your work if it's of a high quality. So, he became a fine artisan, and a smart businessman! As his skills got better, and better, he started to believe that his styles were just about good enough!! Sebastian had seen a number of furniture pieces with an intricate parquetry design, mainly produced in Europe. He was completely enamoured with the fiddly method of workmanship. Once again

Uncle Harold showed him the process.  Sebastian quickly mastered the technique.

He had endless patience, and he needed it! He particularly loved to combine pale English oak and contrasted it with inlaid mahogany. In his eyes, remarkably beautiful. But of course, cedar was to become the main timber of choice as far as he was concerned, oh yes! Or maybe rosewood!

He began, of course, by making various pieces of furniture for the family.  He wisely knew that his mother, who had many friends in the village, would naturally, and proudly, show her neighbours the beautiful and comfortable pieces of furniture. It pays to advertise! His reputation was growing…

Sebastian was just 19 years old when he received his first commissioned order. It was for a solid timber sideboard with Caversham legs, to be manufactured, rather sensibly, from mahogany. Sebastian thought it was an excellent choice. It was ordered by Mr Henry Davidson a wealthy land owner, whose wife had seen the latest cabinet manufactured by Sebastian, whilst visiting  Mrs Hadley.

It should be explained here, that Connie Davidson had two ambitions in life.  One was to keep her little hubby happy, and the other one was to spend as much of his money as she possibly could get her hands on.  Connie gushed over the sideboard until Mr Davidson, in a blur of frustrated uncertainty said: 'Oh alright then, let's buy one of the damned things.'  In actual fact, once Mr Davidson saw the sideboard, he rather sensibly, recognised an artisan of considerable quality… Naturally he thought that he would browbeat Sebastian into making it more cheaply. Mr. Davidson had a lot to learn about Sebastian Rufus Hadley.

Nevertheless, eventually the design was agreed upon, and, after many preliminary sketches were made, a rather beautiful, and detailed drawing was completed by Sebastian showing all the types of timber to be used. Mahogany it was, and damn right too!  Sebastian was far more interested in the style and timber to be used than the cost, but eventually a price was arrived at.  He very boldly, but politely, said that he couldn't predict the completion date. It would take as long as was needed! Mr Davidson warmed to the lad, and a fair price of eight guineas was arrived at. Plus a progress meeting at the Davidson house on a monthly basis,

As Mr. Davidson said: 'there's a drink in it for you'. Sebastian had absolutely no interest in a drink, on a monthly basis, or any other basis for that matter. But would you believe it, Uncle Harold, who attended the meetings had no problem at all in volunteering to keep that part of the bargain.   In fact he graciously and slightly overenthusiastically insisted on being there, monthly, or even more frequently, if necessary.

Oh yes, he actually smiled at the sheer thought of it. Whilst Sebastian explained again that he defiantly couldn't give a certain completion date. Amazingly   enough, Harold enthusiastically nodded his head in total approval, maybe, just maybe, maybe, he knew a thing or two about Mr Davidson.

# CHAPTER FIVE

Over the ensuing months Uncle Harold and Mr. Davies had developed a mutual drinking mate's affection for each other. There was always a plentiful supply of grog at the house and they both enjoyed a glass or two.  Who's kidding whom, they both enjoyed a bottle or three. So, the longer the pesky sideboard took to manufacture… Well you can see where we are going with this can't you!

In fact, on one particular winter's evening the oddest thing happened. During a long and protracted drinking session, they blissfully discovered that they had run out of port. Uncle Harold, who was marginally less pissed than Mr Davies offered to replenish the grog from the kitchen. Now this Friday night was 'bath night'. Mrs Davies, a comely wench, if a soupcon, on the hefty size, was standing in the bath in front of the warm fire, obviously, as naked as the day she was born.

The very inebriated Uncle Harold didn't really bother to knock on the door----he more or less barged in, concentrating on the really important thing, that's it, the port wine. Hence, completely ignoring the nude lady in the bath. On reflection, he rather reasonably said, 'A bottle of port, a bottle of the very, very, fine port.'

Now the good lady, very understandably, seriously thought about screaming, but she quickly realised that Uncle Harold had completely ignored her state of undress, and so, as she coyly held a very small wash cloth in front of her personal floppy bits and pieces—she pointed to the sink and simply said. 'There, port there, port there.'

Like an arrow to a gold mark, Uncle Harold found the bottle and very politely thanked the good lady, in a somewhat flowery way for her unbridled help and staggered back to his drinking pal, all the while guarding the precious bottle as if with his life… Once they had replenished their glasses, first things first, they settled down to imbibe for the rest of the evening.

Mr Davies asked, 'by the by, did you happen to see my wife during your search for the grog'?

Harold thought for quite a long time before gravely answering, 'A pretty girl, a little on the chunky side'?

Mr Davies chortled. 'Yes, yes, that's her alright'.

Uncle, after thinking about it, a great deal answered, 'Yes I think I caught sight of her '.

Mr Davies guffawed a bit. 'Well that's alright then… Fill me up there's a good chap.''

And so it went on, and on, and on.

CHAPTER SIX

Keep your eye on the ball .and present a straight bat.

Sebastian had very few passions in life, outside of his family, and of course, work.

One of his, was the [almost] enormously sensible passion of cricket.

A chess like game, played on a field by white clad folk, over a period of…up to five days.

Sebastian was a bowler of note… fast and with a natural swing to his Yorker.

He was always naturally fit.   He never had to – 'Go for a run', and automatically took on life at a sprint.  So the question of not being ready for a game, never really occurred to him. He was naturally 'up for it'… with bat, or ball in hand. He allowed himself the time off on Saturdays to play for the local team… great fun, and a chance to catch up with his friends… also a break from work.

The cricket club was run by Simon Holyoake. The landlord of the local public house, rather splendidly named The Bell Inn. Mr Holyoake just about ran the whole cricket club from the pub. The practice times, the team players, who would open, etc., etc. He actually selected the team captain. A snotty nosed boy called Howard, whose mother, coincidentally, worked at the hotel. And, amazingly enough, occasionally stayed overnight at the pub. Usually when Mrs Holyoake was away visiting her sister, another coincidence of course!

Make of that what you will, and why not. The rest of the village did! Everyone knew that poor young Howard wasn't that good any batting  or bowling, or fielding, or captaining the side, or anything to do with cricket, for that matter. But his mother smilingly recommended him to Mr Holyoake. So be it.

The reality was, that they hardly ever won a game. Everyone knew why, but they kept their mouths shut. Well, Mr Holyoake did keep a very fine barrel of beer!    In fact, the only source of beer in the village. So! Quite frankly, their occasional sleeping arrangements produced a fair bit of gossip for the village folk.  And you know how people like to go through life… tut tutting.

The team would either celebrate a win, rarely, or commiserate a loss, frequently. But it didn't really matter to Mr Holyoake, because either way, the celebrations were done in his pub. Simon Holyoake was a very smart man!

One of the tasks carried out by the pub was to supply refreshments during the game, or between innings  whichever came first. They were always brought over by Rachel Holyoake, the extremely pretty and curvaceous daughter of the aforementioned Simon.  At the blossoming age of eighteen years, it turned out that Rachel had developed a total disinterest in the game of cricket…However, she had displayed an enthusiastic attraction for all the valiant men in white, in particular, the young, up and coming 'man of the moment'… our Sebastian.

It was even suggested, by some unscrupulous people, who may, or may not, be in the know, that during a short period, whilst Rachel was keeping the score, she hadn't the faintest idea what the rules of the game were, she just might have added a few extra runs onto Sebastian's score... He was an enthusiastic and gallant batsman, but come on, not that good.

What jealous?  Oh please, give us some credit!! Of course, it was just one more, unproven rumour in the village. As previously stressed, tongues will wag you know.

Love actually, not!

 A game of Cricket was, in fact, how the two of them found love. Well, to be more precise, Sebastian discovered it, Rachel was completely unaware of it.  It was a warm June day right in the middle of a game of cricket between their glorious side, and the Gloucester grammar school old boys. Sebastian actually played rather well. He had been promoted up the batting order, and had scored a useful 36 runs. He opened the bowling and took four for eighteen---so his contribution helped them win the match. As he walked of the pitch, Rachel rushed over to him and kissed him on the mouth, and said, 'Well done my little beauty'

Maybe it was her smile more than anything else- but Sebastian's heart literally skipped a beat. He had found unbridled adoration for Rachel. It must be said, in her defence, that she, reasonably innocently, hadn't the faintest idea what all the fuss was about.

Sebastian's life literally changed overnight ........For the first time in his short life, his job, his work, even his mother, became less important by comparison, to 'Rachel the wonderful'. The, as yet, silent passion he felt for another human being was of greater importance than any emotion he had ever endured before. A very typical, if monopolistic attitude, which boys, in particular, seem to wallow in. He was completely, and gloriously lost. Most boys feel this aching pain, at some time or other, but his agony was simply unbearable.

His work suffered---his love of cricket fell apart. Indeed all the vital things in life failed him. His uncle recognised that his, hitherto excellent work, was beginning to suffer. It was literally, not good enough.

Rachel somehow completely understood the power she had over him. She rather condescendingly egged him on, and even made a fool of him, in front of his friends and sporting pals. Only his mother could see what was happening to her son.

Sebastian internalised his feelings, and, on one pivotal day, Saturday the eighteenth of July to be precise, and after scoring a pretty good fifty-nine runs for the team, he found himself walking his treasured one home. Sebastian, plucked up courage and declared his undying love for Rachel. He asked her to marry him! She, slightly indifferently, said she'd think about it. Not quite the answer he was hoping for.

It must be explained here that, at this stage, they had not been intimate. Oddly enough, it was

Rachel who was prepared to go further... Sebastian was in such a conundrum of mixed emotions; he didn't really know what was happening to him. But he was so ridiculously in love with love, that common sense completely deserted him. Ah well, He won't be the first ---- and he unquestionably won't be the last.

The thirteenth of August - a day he will remember for the rest of his life - Rachel, somewhat ungraciously said - YES- YES - YES- YES. Surely the finest word in the often-abused English language. He would never be the same again—all his friends knew that. But love doesn't always listen to reason, and it frequently has a smirk on its face…

# CHAPTER SEVEN

It was a warm day and Sebastian and Rachel had gone down to the river to be by themselves, also to enjoy a picnic next to the cool water. Sebastian almost immediately fell asleep under the willow trees that lined the river bed. It must have been twenty minutes later when he awoke and groggily called out to Rachel. He had no idea where she was.

Then, as he looked over at the river.   Rachel's head bobbed up from the still water… She smilingly asked him to join her for a swim. He shouted out to her that he couldn't because he didn't have his bathing costume with him. Rachel very slowly stood up and nakedly smiled at Sebastian, this was the first time in his life, that he had ever seen a nude girl. She smiled and beckoned for him to him to join her…

He literally sprinted to the water, throwing his clothes off in wild abandon as he staggered and stumbled his way to the river, and, of course, to his beguiling future wife.  The world could have stopped turning. Nothing else mattered.

They consummated their love in the water, then after a while, they consummated it all over again. On the way home, just past farmer Harrison's hay stack, they consummated it again. This consummation business was a bit of alright!!

# CHAPTER EIGHT

Twenty eighth of September, one thirty in the afternoon. His beloved mother was there, his Uncle was there, in a serious and, for him, an uncharacteristically sober mood. Many had conflicting ideas as to the validity of the vows between the soon to be married couple. But Sebastian had always impressed those people who knew him well. Oh yes, he had a wise head on his shoulders for one so young.  Or so they thought.

Any way it's his business so, 'Open the batting and try to score a century', i.e. make the best of it. About three of the boys in the village were sweatily rather pleased that it wasn't they who were standing at the business end of the church. Sebastian's friends, of course attended, as indeed did most of the village folk. Rachel's family was there.  Mr and Mrs Holyoake and Gladys, their youngest daughter, sister of the, soon to be blushing bride.

As Simon Holyoake was obviously at the church, he had temporarily closed the bar, for the very practical reason, that the competition between the church congregation and the pub boozers, was one he couldn't win…so.

They all waited ---and waited----the church clock struck three ominous times! The only one who didn't show up was Rachel. A complete mystery. In a village like Chipping Norton, everyone had private thoughts about the reason for her absence. The three boys, previously mentioned, were apt to keep very quiet about the whole business, they knew a thing or two, or thought they did! Sebastian was shattered, believing of course, that a terrible accident had befallen Rachel. Eventually, after a few days, he was forced to face the agonising truth…

She had simply left him at the altar.

It was another month after that, when he eventually discovered that she had gone to stay with her favourite Aunt Alice in Stroud. Rachel never understood, or in any way cared, just how much devastation and pain she had caused. Neither for that matter did she think tuppence about it. Rachel became a noted stage and music hall actress. As usual, the world got what it deserved. Incidentally she married an equally well noted cabinet minister.

You, of course, know the one I'm talking about.

CHAPTER NINE

Sebastian, utterly shattered though he was, eventually found the strength to pull himself together, but life had changed him completely. He became somewhat more circumspect than he had ever been. A side of his personality that, he himself, didn't like very much—

He sardonically amused himself by calling the period. BR and AR. Easy to work out. Something had to change. It did. After many months of painful and lonely circumspection, he quietly decided to migrate to a new city and try to find a better life. He knew nothing about London, with the exception, that he was aware it was the largest city in the known world.

He was miserable, and frustrated. Anything would be preferable to putting up with walking into a room and hearing the abbreviated conversations coming to an embarrassed and extremely noisy silence! London with all its people, and bright lights sounded just right.   He could easily loose himself in a place that huge. So, London it is!  Ostensibly to find a new life. What he actually wanted was to lose the one he was presently in.

Sebastian knew nothing about London apart from the geography lessons at school. He knew it was pretty big. Probably, even bigger than Stratford. Gosh.

Saying goodbye to his mother was very hard. Oddly enough, his wise mother encouraged him to go to pastures green. She knew her son very well.  His close friends and cricketing team mates were difficult to bid farewell to also, they were his life. He knew no other. Stephen looked everywhere for his Uncle.

The populace of the village all knew he was leaving Chipping Norton.   And they knew why! But Uncle Harold made no effort to contact him. When at last Sebastian tracked him down, inevitably propping up one of the walls in the Bell Inn public house. Sebastian found it difficult, and slightly embarrassing, to speak with his uncle, who didn't turn to look at him, or even acknowledge his shadow. Sebastian, rather naively, had no idea what was wrong. Nevertheless, he duly thanked him for all the affection and guidance he had given him, over the many years they had been together.

Harold didn't even turn around to look at him, he just thrust his hand out and quietly murmured 'Well that's it then. Remember your mother, as she will remember you'. As Sebastian was leaving, he heard his uncle shout out, 'I hadn't finished my lessons to you, there's more -  much more'.

The two men looked at each other for quite a long time. Sebastian just smiled, and then mouthed, 'thank you,' as he left the pub. Nothing else was said.

Harold felt a dreadful emptiness come over him. He dealt with it as he usually did. 'I'll have a large one of those, landlord.' Sebastian had discovered that a stage coach was going up to London in three days' time from Cheltenham spa. He would be on it.

He put everything he needed into a canvas bag, his clothes, all the money that he had amassed over the years, and of course his tools in a separate timber box he made just for the journey. In fact, everything he owned in the world.

# CHAPTER TEN

Goodbye midlands - hello new world!

On the twenty fourth of September Sebastian said goodbye to his Mother. She put her arms around him, and kissed him on both cheeks and ruffled his hair. He slowly said a simple goodbye to his mother.

'I'll be back in about a year mum.' His mother smiled and waved as he left. She knew she would never see him again. Sebastian walked all the way to Cheltenham Spa, a place he had been to before, but only as a child, and hence he had no recollections of the town. His mind was elsewhere. He arrived at Queen's hotel in the middle of town early in the morning, only to be told that the stagecoach was running late. He would have to wait at least another three days before joining the carriage…

Sebastian was not a person to panic about time, or anything else, for that matter. So, he made himself as comfy and as cheaply as he could, by sleeping under the rotunda bandstand near the town centre. Well, it was dry and relatively warm. The cold of winter had not descended from the heavens as yet. Thus, he was cosy - well as cosy as anyone could be in Cheltenham.

He thought seriously about walking all the way to London, but decided it was too far to travel with his bag of clothes; but, particularly his precious tools.   They were part of his plans to start a new life… Sebastian knew his worth, so naturally assumed that he would get work fairly easily, find good digs and, maybe bring his Mother up to London.  She would enjoy seeing the largest city in the world.

Yes, yes, a new life for her would be perfect. Of course, he had no idea what his mother might think of this. So here he was in Cheltenham. Nothing much happens in Cheltenham, nothing ever does, really.  So, nothing to report here.

The coach rumbled into the town centre at seven o clock in the morning. It looked heroically glamorous in its weather-beaten maroon colours, with 'Midlands to London' emblazoned on it. Shame it was so bloody uncomfortable.

The price to get up to London was two shillings…an absolute fortune…. But what can you do? He was to share the journey with six other passengers. All of them looked cold and miserable. Sebastian politely removed his hat and said good morning. Not one of them answered him, surly buggers! It was going to be a long trip.

Once they had passed the relatively straight and flattened roads around Cheltenham, they found themselves at the mercy of the bumpy, and boulder strewn tracks, on the way to the next town, which was a picturesque little village called Burford. The most totally dreary place in the world, to everyone, apart from the good folk who lived in Burford, of course. Then on to Oxford, a remarkably beautiful city, and, one of the oldest university towns in the world. And big!! Yes. Oh yes. BIG. Sebastian began to realise that maybe Stratford wasn't all that large after all. Of course, compared to Chipping Norton it was. He wondered if London was even bigger!

At Oxford they all had to wait for three hours so that a new set of horses could be harnessed to the coach. All of the passengers were given a chance to stretch their legs. They stayed at the 'Pilgrims Inn' which was warm and comfortable and very welcoming. Sebastian took the opportunity to order a ploughman's lunch, without the beer or cider of course.

He got chatting to one of his fellow passengers who told him that he was a sales man, travelling in ladies under clothing. Sebastian stared at him for a moment, gosh that's an odd thing to admit to, but he looked alright. Suppose! His name was Gerald Smyth. He told Sebastian that he knew London pretty well and warned him to give the East end a wide berth - they were a very common, and rather distasteful group of vagabonds. 'Watch them like a hawk.' said the man who travelled in ladies' bloomers. Gerald Smyth recommended he head for Golders green. A fine quiet area, where everyone is welcome. Well my friend. You can always trust a Jew. So wrote another Jew.

## CHAPTER ELEVEN

Welcome to the capital of capitals.

They arrived in London on Friday afternoon. London wasn't big, it was bloody enormous. They travelled for nearly another day before they reached Golders Green.

Sebastian was, in some ways, very lucky.  He had met a number of Jewish people whilst in Chipping Norton, and, had always found them to be straight forward and basically very honest. Also, they seemed to have the most marvellous, self-depreciating sense of humour, 'so my dears', what's not to like! In fact, it was the Jewish people who helped him to develop an attitude of 'Easy come, easy go'.

So, Golders Green, whilst not known to him, held very little fear. Within two days he had met a Mr Henri Spielmann, who ran the family second hand furniture shop in the outskirts of Golders Green. Henri Spielmann quickly offered him a job, 'But on a trial basis only, if your work didn't meet with my work practices. Out, you go.''

Sebastian  nodded understandingly, and walked about the shop.  He checked quite a few pieces of the furniture he saw dotted around the place, and smiled to himself. The tables and chairs etc., were simply not, in any way, near his exacting qualities of workmanship.  A wage was agreed upon and he could live in the workshop, clean and warm, what else could you want! For the first time in his life. Sebastian pondered if his work standards were aiming, in fact, too high. That had never crossed his mind before. He would obviously have to prove himself.

 Well.... That was just fine! It turned out that Henri Spielmann was of a similar age to Sebastian, but so what. As long as the furniture he sold made a good profit---what else mattered? But it would most certainly 'matter' to his 'Saturday morning' friends, people who would pay for, 'Class, my dear'.  At the synagogue, no less.

Obviously, this meant absolutely nothing to Sebastian.  He had very quickly found a simple and viable way of life in London that suited him down to the ground. His mantra was hard work will set you free! So, just do it!

Henri Spielmann, very quickly realised that he was developing a new, classier, and much wealthier clientele from in and around London, and in particular, of course Golders Green.

He would never admit it, but a major part of his success, was down to Sebastian's growing reputation as an artisan of genuine quality.  Of course, Sebastian also gained as he was able to produce timber furniture which he considered acceptable to his demanding standards. So everyone profited, my dears. A Yiddish philosophy.

Sebastian and Henri discovered, that in some ways, they were very similar, both were young, both were prepared to work hard for what they wanted, even if neither of them was exactly sure what that was. But In rational terms, that's pretty much where the similarities ended. Henri's main priority in life, was that the absolute necessity to please his family - especially his mother. Virtually nothing else even mattered to him. Whereas Sebastian only had to please the man he looked at whilst he shaved in the morning. Well, it wasn't quite that simple. He found that he was having to come to terms with the reality, that he was a loner! Obvious really! However, they both enjoyed the friendship they shared, to a large degree, brought about by a similar sense of rather childish humour. Even though their lifestyles were so vastly different, it was a friendship that was excellent - but for different reasons…

Sebastian was entirely happy by himself, with the proviso that he had a piece of furniture to work on. Whilst Henri enjoyed being surrounded with friends, especially those at the synagogue who were, not only very influential but - in the know! They were aware of everything that was going on, especially in the city. Not all of it strictly legitimate, but that didn't seem to worry them all that much. Henri said, 'just turn a blind eye and a deaf ear my friend'. Jewish people had a way with words!

All Sebastian wanted to do was make a living in a world that seemed quite alien to his past life in Chipping Norton. He had a very simple attitude to life.  His background, and upbringing in the small farming community, promoted a black or white attitude. It turned out that Henri was quite generous with his money. So as per usual, everyone gained. Again, the Jewish way.

Sebastian saw no reason not to keep up his level of fitness; so going for a daily run around the Temple Park was completely normal to him. He was fit and strong and hardly ever walked anywhere, running was better, he really wasn't fast. He actually loped his way through life. Henri watched him occasionally, and decided he was as mad as a hatter! But then, neither of them cared what the other thought, so it didn't matter, did it! Henri was a man who liked to talk---in fact it was difficult shut him up at times, he told Sebastian about some of the influential people he had got to know at the synagogue. One of them was a doctor named Dr Esau Abraham, a brilliant man, and a practicing heart specialist, still only 38 years old. It turned out that Dr Abraham wasn't all that much of a talker, which, of course, suited Henri down to the ground. Thank heavens, like most doctors he was a splendid intuitive listener. It turned out that Dr Abraham was becoming, not just a fine and well-respected specialist in Harley Street, but a man of great influence in the city. It was obvious, from the way that Henri talked about Dr Abraham, that he was an exceptionally impressive man, one that you would want on your side in a sticky situation. Oh, if only the fellow played cricket!

# CHAPTER TWELVE.

A lifelong friendship starts with a smile.

Sebastian allowed himself a couple of hours a week away from work. He loved walking around London. He was constantly amazed at the size of the buildings, and the endless numbers of people. Throngs, and yet, more throngs of them. All of them seemingly busy, but aimlessly dashing about, most of them aggressively gesticulating and non-stop talking, yes chattering constantly- and to whom? Sebastian was somewhat amused at the expressions on their faces! He couldn't imagine what they had to say to each other, all the time. Maybe that's where Henri gets it from!

On one of his walks, Sebastian found himself outside the synagogue that Henri attended. It was late on Saturday afternoon and a delightfully warm sunny day. Life is made up of extraordinary coincidences. This was undoubtedly one of them! Henri, came out of the synagogue, a grey rather unspectacular building from the outside, inevitably talking to Dr Abraham, as usual, Henri was doing most of the chattering. Sebastian watched and smiled to himself, entirely aware that his friend would commandeer most of the air space between them. What was equally obvious, was that Dr Abraham was asking occasional, poignant questions, and in general, seemed to be getting the answers he sought.

Henri saw Sebastian and beckoned him over to meet with Dr Abraham. Sebastian, very carefully, made his way across the busy road, dodging carriages, bicycles, and of course, the inevitable people. Sebastian was surprised to be introduced by Henri, in a somewhat light hearted way as: 'My good friend the country bumpkin, Sebastian.' Dr Abraham smiled and told Sebastian that he had heard a lot about him from Henri. Sebastian returned the smile and shook his hand. He was surprised to find the doctor had a very strong hand grip. Sebastian absorbed the steady gaze of the Doctor and decided, there and then, that this was a man to trust. Dr Abraham smilingly asked Sebastian what his passion was, a slightly odd question but… Sebastian stoically answered, 'I manufacture the finest furniture it is possible to buy anywhere. All the pieces are bespoke and made to order.' As an afterthought he added, 'of course I also repair some of Henri's s--- stuff. There was not a hint of braggart in his comments. He honestly knew it to be the truth. He saw Dr Abraham smile, but then he gravely nodded and said. 'It is important to have faith in your own talents, if you don't believe, who will? It was a pleasure to meet you. I hope you will forgive my leaving you, but I have a great deal of reading to catch up on.' As he turned to leave, he stopped and added, 'I feel sure that we will meet again. Good day to you both.'

Henri chattered most of the way home. He told Sebastian that he had mentioned to  Dr Abraham just how splendid his furniture was. Sebastian smilingly said, 'Oh if I'd known how much you liked my work, I'd have asked you for more money.' Henri immediately changed his tune and lost his sense of humour.

'You're not all that good boyo, not that good at all.'

Sebastian just smiled at him and said, 'Don't worry, I'll work for you till something else comes along. In the meantime, you should know that I'm grateful for the start you've given me'. Henri immediately started talking about something else. As usual asking questions of himself and then, of course, answering them.

Sebastian smiled all the way home. In turn it was obvious that Henri admired Sebastian. In particular his innate sense of right and wrong. You knew where you stood with Sebastian... Not always the case with Henri… Ah well, he wasn't all bad.

# CHAPTER THIRTEEN.

It was a bitterly cold Wednesday afternoon, a good day for hard work.

Sebastian was putting the finishing touches on a mahogany sideboard that had been commissioned by a client of Henri.

All of the timber had to be French polished--- extremely important as far as Sebastian was concerned. It was an arduous task that took a great deal of concentration. Only small areas could be tackled at any one time.

It had to be right, that's all there was to it!

At least it kept you warm!

Dr Abraham had called to visit Henri's  parents. By sheer coincidence neither Henri, nor his folks were at home that day.  But he did hear the most awful caterwauling coming from the workshop. Intrigued, he walked over to see who was intentionally murdering 'A wandering Minstrel' with such ghastly off tone, screechy whistles. Obviously, it was Sebastian.

The Doctor watched him work.

Over the short period Sebastian had  inhabited the planet, he had developed the most extraordinary capacity to concentrate on his work.   It was like a religion to him; nothing would get in his way.

 He finished the small part of the cabinet he was working on, before he even realised that the Doctor was watching him. When he did become aware, he abruptly stopped and politely went over to the Doctor and said 'I'm  sorry, but I didn't see you.  I'm afraid that I get so absorbed in my work that bombs could go off and I'd miss them - that's supposed to be a joke –I don't like bombs, by the way.'

The doctor smiled and mentioned.  'Who in their right mind does?'  Sebastian nodded and said, 'I don't believe that either Henri or his parents are at home presently.'

Abraham nodded as he walked around the cabinet and, without saying a word, gently eased out one of the drawers, it neither wobbled or made the slightest noise as he pushed it back in place, to where it would be for the next hundred years, or more.

The Doctor very quietly said, 'my father used to be a carpenter in Poland, his work was very fine, but not in the same league as yours.' 'It's no wonder that Henri speaks so highly of you. Yours is a special talent, not just your superb workmanship, but I watched you for ten minutes, and, apart from your completely tuneless whistling, I could see that you were utterly absorbed in your 'piece of fun.'

The well-mannered Sebastian bristled slightly and started to contradict the doctor.

'Excuse me Doctor Abraham but I think that you misunderstand me, this- bit of fun - as you call it, is my life's work.  This is how I---'

Dr Abraham smiled and interrupted Sebastian by saying, 'Please understand me, my sense of humour is very Jewish, actually it was supposed to be a compliment to you, or at least, that's how it sounded in my head.

I must tell you that Henri talks about you a lot, frankly he never seems to stop talking, about everything, and nothing, another little joke, but I can see what he means.' Abraham paused. 'Your furniture is beautiful and most impressive and your work ethics seem to be, there is no other phrase that I can think of, faultless.'

Sebastian answered without smiling. 'I had the finest teacher you can imagine; he was everything to me, a friend, teacher, a father figure and a taskmaster. I was a lucky man.'

Abraham rather gravely said. 'Maybe you were both lucky. Please tell Henri that I called. I will see you again, I'm sure of it.'

He didn't say goodbye, he didn't need to. It was as if he surrounded himself with knowledge---without actually saying anything.

# CHAPTER FOURTEEN.

A new direction. Go north young man!

Over the ensuing six months, Dr Abraham found his way to the furniture store on a regular basis. He always made time to visit Sebastian in his work place. He simply got pleasure out of watching Sebastian ply his trade. The man was worthy of admiration!

Dr Abraham usually tried to get to the workshop round about tea time three o'clock in the afternoon, a very civilised period and so unquestionably Bulldoggish.

Dr Abraham could be very amusing as he told protracted stories about his family. They had migrated to all parts of the world. The doctor told stories of the adventures they had in darkest Africa, unbelievably hot and sticky. And the wildlife! Africa was still a relatively new country- at least to the British, they still had much to learn about new domains.

Dr Abraham, in many ways, was not unlike Sebastian.  They both shared a remoteness that was a natural part of their personality. But the doctor was much more inquisitive. For instance, he frequently asked Sebastian about himself; where he came from, if his mother still lived in the same village, where the rest of his family lived, if they were still alive.

When he heard that Sebastian's Father had died, all those years ago. He wanted to know, how it happened, and what caused his demise… Firstly, Sebastian didn't know and, secondly, he couldn't understand why the doctor was that interested anyway. Altogether, rather worrying!

It merits saying that Sebastian wrote to his mother each month, and had done since moving to London. Gillian was surprised as to why a Doctor in London was so interested about state of health of her son's family. Nevertheless, she answered as best she could, with as much medical detail as she could remember.

January in England could be very cold. This year wasn't just cold, it was bloody freezing. Sebastian was never worried about the cold weather. All he did was put on another pair of gloves that his mother had knitted for him. They were all he needed. He was tough!

On a typical Friday afternoon, Sebastian was working away, as usual, wearing his new gloves. Naturally he was completely engrossed in his work. He ignored Dr Abraham, not out of ill manners. He literally had no idea that the doctor was standing just ten yards away, watching him. Dr Abraham smiled and carried on his way to the main house.

THE PASSOVER.

Henri explained to Sebastian that they probably wouldn't be seeing much of Dr Abraham for quite a while. It was the sacred celebration of Passover and nearly all orthodox Jewish people observed

The celebration, which began on the fourteenth day of Nisan and lasts for eight days.

So, it was most unusual to find Dr Abraham in the middle of the festival outside the workshop. As per usual he was watching Sebastian work.

The Doctor very gravely said, 'I had to see you, I wouldn't be here if it wasn't important.'

Sebastian, utterly confused, looked the doctor in the eyes, then spoke from his heart. 'Doctor Abraham, it's time for me to tell you that I have been very confronted by all the extremely personal questions you have asked of me. I'm a straightforward man, so, right now, tell me what this is all about!'

Dr Abraham nodded his head and haltingly addressed Sebastian. 'I am quite aware that you must be confused, and again, I apologise if you have ever thought I was being underhanded. There is nothing that you should concern yourself with at this moment, or any moment –if it comes to that.'

The doctor stared Sebastian in the face and explained. 'I have a proposition to put to you, but, quite frankly, at the moment, I have to keep the details secret. I trust that you know me well enough to believe that I have your interests at heart. Believe me, this will change your life forever, and in a good way.' The Doctor continued. 'There are a number of people who will want to meet you, but, that will need to wait for a short time more. I apologise in advance for all the secrecy, and, I sincerely hope that I have said enough to galvanise the creative juices in your fertile mind. But, for the time being. I bid you goodbye.'

He shook Sebastian's hand and turned on his heels and left as abruptly as he arrived.

Henri poked his head around the door. It was obvious that he had been eavesdropping, to say that Henri was a most complex man would be a massive understatement. He frequently accompanied Dr Abraham into the workshop and seemed engrossed, not by the work that Sebastian was doing, but more, by the somewhat private conversations between Sebastian and Doctor Abraham. In fact, none of Henri's business.

It crossed Sebastian's mind, that it was almost as though Henri was jealous of his friendship with Dr Abraham. That made absolutely no sense, but why? Dr Abraham was Henri's friend and spiritual advisor, so he decided. Not my bloody business anyway.

Sebastian quietly made up his mind that he would get on with his work and wait for something better to turn up.

# CHAPTER FIFTEEN

Something better turned up.

Less than a week later he received a letter from Dr Abraham.  It was brought in by Henri, who virtually threw it on the bench and refused to look at Sebastian. He started to leave, then turned round and stared at Sebastian before saying. 'I suppose that means you'll be leaving now!'

The expression on his face was a mixture of anger and contempt.  'You don't have to explain, it's been bloody obvious for at least a month.'

Sebastian slowly walked over to Henri. 'I want you to listen to me, I haven't the faintest idea what this about, but I'd like you stand here and listen to me as I read it.'

He opened the embossed envelopes and read the contents whilst Henri waited.  Right, here we are. It's not a job offer, he wishes to meet with me to introduce his business friends, so it's not in any way what you thought it to be.'

Henri started to speak but Sebastian stopped him by holding up his hand.

'I have absolutely no idea what this means  but, I want you to know that. I have been aware of your mounting animosity to me.'

He waited a moment before continuing, and smiled as he explained. 'Henri, I appreciate that you gave me a job and a place to live. I will always be grateful to you, and your family for the kindness you showed me, but I cannot live my life around unfounded suspicions. I still have no idea what this letter means, but I must tell you that I intend to find out. I don't really understand it myself, and I find it difficult to explain to you. But I must follow my nose to whatever adventure is out there. I wish to see the world and, taste all the fruits.' He smiled as he explained. 'Even if some of them are sour, so.  I will go along to meet with the Doctor.  I hope that you understand'

Henri stared at Sebastian for a while and then, extraordinarily enough said nothing.  Just turned on his heels and disappeared.

It was less than two weeks before Dr Abraham called at the Spielmann's home.   He spent over an hour with Henri before making his way to the workshop. He opened the door and said. 'If you're not doing anything next Friday, I'd be extremely grateful if you could join us at the address on this letter. It will explain, at least some of the questions that I feel certain you want answers to. By the way, maybe you could talk to Henri, I suspect that you'll find that he's a good and honest friend. I do apologise, again for all this secrecy, once we have explained the subject, and all its complexity, I hope you'll understand.'

He walked over to Sebastian and rather gravely shook his hand, then immediately left.

Sebastian went back to his French polishing.

His instincts told him that he needed to finish the sideboard as quickly as possible…

# CHAPTER SIXTEEN

New friends —new directions.

The address on the embossed envelope was in a place named, 'Piccadilly Circus'.

Sebastian had never heard of it, but he made the wise decision not to walk there especially if one doesn't know where it is. But he discovered that it was possible to get a stagecoach service almost to the door. But the cost. Six pence. Well, maybe just this once.

He arrived at the enormous house at two minutes past four o-clock in the afternoon. He knocked on the front door and was relieved to find Dr Abraham waiting for him. The doctor smiled at Sebastian and ushered him into the huge parlour. Sebastian very quickly, took in the preassembled host of people, all of them males, and, most of them a similar age to himself.

They were all very friendly and welcoming.

Abraham stayed close to Sebastian and helped to make him feel like a crony amongst new pals. A butler gave him a cup of tea and ushered him to a seat.

It was obvious to Sebastian that they all knew each other. He put his teacup and saucer on the small table next to the chair. It wasn't particularly well made, it wobbled, a lot.

Dr Abraham smiled as he watched Sebastian test the table his expression said everything! Sebastian became aware that most of the men were observing him, not in a guinea pig sort of way ---but as another fellow human being.

At last Abraham held up his hand and addressed Sebastian personally. 'It's time for me to explain myself, and the reason we have asked you to join us. Predominantly, we are a group of scientists, geologists, climatologists, civil engineers and very ordinary doctors, like myself.'

He paused before continuing by announcing. 'We intend to form the very first group of adventurers who will travel to the —as yet, unexplored North Pole. Let me assure you that it's very easy to say that, nestled as we are, in this warm and safe environment, but incredibly trying in reality. And, I must admit to you, a dangerous task at that.'

He continued. 'All the people here are involved, and all have varying qualities to offer. I will, of course, introduce you to them, one by one.' He smiled at Sebastian as he spoke.

'I fully expect that you will discover that they are all scallywags---but, in every case, utterly reliable and completely trustworthy.'

The Doctor intoned. 'You may well ask, what reason I have to nominate you to this bunch of rascals. Well, now is the time to tell you----For the last few months, I have been observing you – I see in you, the qualities that would help to bring this group of such divergent men together.

You are practical and hardworking to the point of obsession, obviously your fitness is also paramount. Frankly, you will need to go through some stringent medical checks, including dental assessments. So, it's very simple. We can't offer anything to you, other than hard work and adventure. But I can promise that you'll come back a different person. Well I've done all the talking so far, and I must tell you that, apart from your 'ghastly whistling,' I think you would fit in very well. Right, it's now your turn.'

Sebastian looked at the amassed group of men for a while, then said, 'The table you served my tea on is wobbly, it needs fixing.'

The adventurers smiled at him and began to realise that he was a bit of character, and a reliable one at that. Dr Abraham had voiced what the rest of them were thinking, this was a fine and worthy man.  If only he was a magnetationist.

Sebastian had never heard of the phrase, so he just nodded his head and explained that, he wouldn't know it if he tripped over one, so.

The doctor explained that they were in great need of a specialist to locate, and, ultimately, establish the precise   position of the magnetic north pole; and with it, naturally, claim it as a Great Britain protectorate. Of course.

The next three months were truly frenetic for Sebastian, he was constantly asked to meet at the Piccadilly Circus House.  Very thoughtfully, they now provided transport and, at last, he was able to understand what an enormous place London really was. The committee asked him to be at the address by about five o-clock in the evening if possible.

On one occasion the transport didn't turn up. Sebastian waited till four thirty. No transport. At last, he decided to run all the way there.

He set off running at a steady lope. He knew the way pretty well by then. Sebastian arrived at the house only ten minutes later than specified. He took an enormous deep breath and knocked on the massive portal.

The door was opened by the butler who ushered him into the main office.

All the usual men were there, and it must be said that they were all smiling. Dr Abraham offered his hand and welcomed him into the room. Sebastian started to explain that the transport hadn't arrived, so.

Dr Abraham held up his hand and said. 'I trust that you will forgive me, but this was just one more test to, well frankly, to analyse your initiative, and by the way, you passed with flying colours.'

Abraham smilingly said. 'No one expected you to run all the way, I'm not even sure that anyone else would be so enthusiastic to be here exactly on time.' Sebastian smiled at the amassed company and explained to them. 'You obviously didn't play cricket for Chipping Norton.   If you were late twice, you were dropped, gentlemen, I was never late.'

The very vociferous crowd were mostly laughing, some just smiled, mainly cricketers.

All were delighted by the natural charm of the man. Doctor Abraham very gravely said, 'I'm sure that, by now, you realise that we have been assessing you over these last few months, we have arrived at a unilateral conclusion.'

He almost stiffened as he rather formally proclaimed: 'Sebastian Rufus Hadley, we would like to offer you a place in our party to travel to as yet, undiscovered lands; in and around the North Pole of the Northern Hemisphere, in fact we endeavour to be the first party to actually map and establish exactly where the pole is. There are, of course, many plans that we need to advise you of. But in the meantime,' Dr Abraham stood up and spoke rather formally, 'Please join us in a toast to, our successful and safe adventure, and our return to the safety of mother England.'

Sebastian was aware that all the men were congratulating him and shaking his hand. He was in a complete whirl. The butler came in with an enormous tray of drinks. They all took a drink and turned to Sebastian and toasted him. 'Your health sir.'

Sebastian stood up and answered by saying. 'Thank you, sirs for this great honour, but, I want you to understand that I am a confirmed non-drinker, but I would love a cup of tea, milk with no sugar. Oh, and don't put it on that table until I have repaired it properly.'

The whole party was amused at the ridiculousness of the comment, each man lifted his glass, with the obvious exception of teetotal Sebastian, and toasted the exciting future.

Naturally they were all  in high spirits  as they talked about the adventures about to engulf them.

*********************

It was the start of many toil-filled days, where their friendships became less alien and more closely trusting of each other. Each man had specific attributes, quite apart from their academic qualifications. It would appear that, two of the men were expert dog handlers. All of the team were made aware of how important the animals were.  In simple terms the Canadian husky dogs will be their only means of transport.

Without the dogs the expedition would have absolutely no chance of survival. Every one of the men knew that the dogs were their life blood.

Two men were in charge of organising the food for both the men and the dogs Sebastian was delighted to learn, that it was different for each. It was estimated that each man would need approximately three pounds of food per day. Of course, in their innocence, they all believed that the area would supply them with basic food. From the natural fauna, fish, penguins, and of course bird's eggs. They had absolutely no idea!

Sebastian was beginning to understand just what he had taken on! His main task would be to build a very basic timber hut.  It would be tantamount to their survival, and at least as important as anything else. He was able to estimate how large the hut would need to be. He decided to design it, and cut the timber to size whilst still in England. Somewhat like a prefabricated unit.

Dr Abraham saw Sebastian's plans, and, with the acceptance of the other men, the plan was endorsed. All the other men had similar tasks to prepare for. The geologists, the engineers and, at last they had met a magnetologist who was young and keen to prove his theories about magnetic susceptibilities.

Sebastian's excitement grew every day. Dr Abraham suggested that he should consider writing to his family in the midlands and explain that he would be absent for a while. He wrote to his Mother and tried to explain the marvellous adventure about to happen to him.

A similar letter was penned to his uncle Harold. He tried to explain all the things that catapulted into his mind; Dr Abraham advised not to give too much detail because it was of such a technical, and in some ways, a secret nature. He considered writing to Rachel but realised, at last, that his life had taken a totally different path. She was simply a closed chapter in his life.

# CHAPTER   SEVENTEEN

Don't waste a single day of your life.

The departure for the North Pole was planned for the nineteenth of March.  It was presumed that the journey would take about six to eight weeks to travel to the landing place called Koorangle Bay. Prior to leaving, each member had to submit to stringent fitness and health checks, including a dental examination of teeth.  Whilst it was accepted that Dr Abraham was a brilliant physician and practical doctor, with many years' experience, the physical examinations graphically reminded all of them of the dangers they faced.  However, in many ways it helped to bring them together. They saw themselves as a bunch of intrepid adventurers, which was precisely what they were.

Doctor Abraham, who, armed with his creative sense of humour, drew up a statistical medical diary for everyone.

He drew little pictures of all the participants, showing amusing strengths and weaknesses. He included himself in this. If nothing else, at least he was democratic.

Sebastian's apparent weakness was that he could never stop talking about cricket. As far as he was concerned cricket, was a fine and intelligent game, played by, white clad gentlemen against other equally white clad gentlemen. A splendid game. And so say all of us! Well at least Sebastian.

The history of the desire to explore and conquer the North Pole is, as ancient as it is unfathomable. It was believed that the Vikings had ventured to the actual area a number of times, but even those intrepid souls were unprepared for the extraordinary conditions that all explorers face. It must have been a shock for those gallant adventurers. It was believed that at least five times the Viking parties, tried to make land there, they were never heard of, or seen again.

This was the first of the English expeditions, and backed by some very powerful and well-known people from banking circles in the city. The party was   prepared very professionally, and all the anticipated problems had been carefully discussed, and hopefully, resolved.

It was generally decided to take very small steps. The first being to establish a small, but hopefully, permanent settlement. It would act as a communication base, and, sort of a physiological home structure.

Sebastian though not a builder, had been chosen to select timber for the log cabin. It was understood that it would be a solid and basic hut with no windows but designed with two opposing doors. Of course, all this was decided upon in front of a warm fire in Jolly Old England. At the time it all seemed very feasible and eminently achievable. Most plans do under those circumstances.

# CHAPTER EIGHTEEN

The nineteenth of March turned out to be a relatively warm early spring day. A fine time to start the adventure of a life time. The intrepid H.M.S Reliance left London Town from the port of Greenwich at three  thirty in the morning. It was unilaterally decided not to indulge in an official send off.

This was essentially a Geographical  Expedition. They sailed up the North Sea and into the vast Norwegian fiords. Needless to say, it didn't take long before the icy weather reminded them of the anticipated hardships of the mission. It was an important time in which they would get used to the special clothing they would have to wear from now on. It was also the time to take the chance to become friends with the husky dogs, a singularly beautiful animal and, in most cases, quite friendly. They were of course, reminded that the animals were the only means of transport they had.  But, more importantly, they were a sort of spiritual connection.

As they gazed out to the relentless northern sea, they faced their first taste of really cold weather. They were all used to icy weather in England and some had worked in Scotland. So surely nothing could be colder than the Orkney Islands in winter. Especially when the temperature dropped to minus fifteen degrees. That's cold laddie, really cold. They had no idea!!

They arrived at Koorangle Bay on the first of April.  No one had the temerity to point out the light-hearted meaning of the day. They simply had far too much to do.

Everything had to be unloaded from the HMS Reliance as quickly as possible and stacked in the most convenient location. The Reliance had orders to return to active duty as soon as this mission was safely escorted to the bay.

They were all aware that their sleeping accommodation had been specially manufactured and designed from green canvas.  The tents were very strong, with double thickness wall material. That would keep the cold out!

The unloading of the food took on a major priority, everything had to be stacked in piles so that it was available when needed.  The one thing they didn't have to concern themselves with was keeping the meat cold. On the, contrary, the main worry was being able to get at it, within a very few days it was covered in nearly a metre's thickness of ice.

The timber for the hut took on secondary priority, but would in fact be the saviour of the party as soon as it was completed. Amazingly the dogs seemed to acclimatise quite quickly. They were the toughest of the tough. They were extraordinarily lucky in that the weather was not all that bad.  Whilst the temperature was exceptionally cold, the terrifying wind hadn't shown its scary self as yet.

The party immediately prioritised the building of the hut, Sebastian took charge of the construction of the simple shanty. It had to be completed, that's all there was to it.

He proved his value in more ways than his building abilities. He became a natural leader and a source of inspiration to the other men, always the first to start work.   He somehow understood completely that the hut was vital to their survival, the hut had to be completed before the weather changed.

Some of the men were able to take in the awesomely imposing landscape. The mountains of ice were so incredible they were shocked by their enormous size.  The colours screeched from pale blue to the darkest purple and pitch black in the foreboding shadows. Incredibly beautiful, whilst at the same time terrifying.

If the men were starting to feel the pressure of the tasks in front of them, they stoically kept their fears to themselves. At this time of year, for a very short time, it never got dark, however they were entirely aware that the winter would bring on nearly perpetual darkness. They had pre-bargained that the food they had brought with them would last until they could catch local food, fish, penguins, seals etc., etc.

They hadn't the faintest idea what they were doing.  It was the wrong season, which meant that no natural fauna was available. Innocent disaster! Most of the food they brought with them was rationed out at, two pounds of vitals per day, per person, mostly dried meat, hard tack biscuits and ground cocoa with small amounts of sugar and grain in the form of rolled oats.

The dogs also had to exist on very meagre rations. They all expected it to be tough but, secretly this was a shock to their untutored expectations. Physiologically they were still strong and resilient, but they had never faced cold weather like this, and the winds. My God the start of the winds was inconceivable, nothing could have prepared them for this.

Somehow Sebastian just carried on with the inevitable building, nothing seemed to stop him. He even whistled, tunelessly of course, as he got on with his job. During the times when the wind reduced its intensity, they took the chance to take in the soaring cliffs of solid ice. They were so gigantic that, they seemed to completely disorient the compasses that they brought with them, which in turn appeared to make them unreadable, the pointers indicating different positions of the North Pole.

One of the things that must be mentioned, Polar Bears, they were enormous. They had, of course, heard of them, but they had absolutely no idea how massive they were. The pictures they had seen of them in London, somehow made them look friendly and somewhat cuddly. The reality was that they were frighteningly vicious...especially if they were hungry, and they were nearly always ravenous. It was, after all their environment, and the bears coped with it very well. But blimey the size!

They seemed to live on the lower slopes, but a hungry bear is an absolutely terrifying proposition. Sebastian had never killed a wild animal in his life. But he conceded that if he, of his companions were threatened, he would fire the rifle he had with him at all times. They had all been advised during the meetings in London, that in extremely simple terms you must shoot to kill. A wounded bear is a dangerous proposition.

We were lucky the dogs' barking kept us aware if a bear was in the vicinity. And we always had at least two men on guard in case of emergency. Sebastian proved to be a valiant force of hopeful fun. On one day as the wind dropped its intensity, he got the men together and divided them into two teams to play, of course, a game of cricket.  It helped to lift their spirits, it also it warmed them up a bit. An ice breaker in every way. Again, cricket to the rescue!!

Ten days later the hut was finished, basic as it was, with two doors, each one on a diagonally opposite wall. It was enough to house all the men, and of course, give them a tiny bit of warmth and protection. Also, the dogs were able to take shelter and derive some warmth from the formidable  cold.

It was party time; the men felt the need to celebrate for the first time since embanking on the frozen wasteland.    They were destined to sleep in relative comfort. Until this time it had proved impossible to light the kerosene lamps, let alone keep them alight, so that food could be cooked. They had existed on frozen provisions. Now at last they could actually cook some food and close a door.  What a luxury.

They had all but forgotten the basics. That night they dined on cooked, well, semi dried meat with a ration of biscuits and WARM COCOA.  A feast in any other terms. The dogs were also given a treat as they snuggled down to canine luxury.

Nearly all the men descended into, what amounted to juvenile histrionics, but that was simply an indication of the tension they had all been under since they had landed on the damned place. They were very aware that Sebastian's building effort was the main provider of their present, relative comfort. The hut had changed their lives in a wonderful way. They decided to celebrate the building of the hut with a party.

But life is never that simple.

Jonas Seagram had gone out to check on the dogs. He came back and rather joylessly reported that there was an eerie silence outside.  In fact, they had never heard the deadly silence as it presented itself to the partiers.

The lifted spirits of the men argued their way into a celebration.  Dr Abraham gave each of the men a substantial tot of single malt whiskey to toast the success of the construction.

The men were laughing and joking as they ate the gastronomic delights set before them. Sebastian declined the whiskey, obviously, but he enjoyed the camaraderie of his friends. He relaxed for the first time since he had completed the hut. Jonas and another of the engineers surreptitiously, and jokingly, poured an enormous tot of whiskey into Sebastian's mug of cocoa whilst he wasn't looking.

They all toasted one another by lifting their glasses, including the usually innocent alcohol-free Sebastian. He joined in with his new friends and downed the full mug of cocoa in one gulp.

It was the last thing he remembered for ever.

He literally passed out exactly where he was sitting. The rest of the men thought it was a marvellous joke. They all drank the pure whiskey and fell deeply into an alcohol coma. None of them heard the monumental roar as the blizzard hurled across the plain. The wind blew at over one hundred and fifty miles an hour.

It blew everything in its path away, including the hut, which buckled like Vesta match sticks. Every man, every dog, every vestige of their being there, was blown into a crevasse at least two hundred yards deep, and covered with literally thousands of tonnes of pure ice.

Sebastian, still in a firmament of drunkenness, tumbled into the snow and landed without a scratch, protected by the liquid he had always baulked against. The uncaring snow fell on top of him, and covered him in a cocoon of minus fifty degrees ice, never to move again.

No one could possibly survive in those conditions.

************************************

# PART TWO.

## CHAPTER ONE.

The best of today, is tomorrow.

The fourteenth of September.    The year twenty fifteen.

 The usually reliable weather forecast promised a ten-day window of acceptable conditions, not ideal.  But…

It was now, or wait another eighteen months, this time, the powers that be said yes. It was as simple as that. Twelve months of careful planning had gone into this expedition, it was very expensive, dangerous, and often, unfortunately, less than productive.

The U.E.S Exploration Society had expressed, very strongly, that they did not have endless capital and that the committee members would expect to see some viable proof to justify the expenses. They were told, in no uncertain terms, that funds were not, by any means, inexhaustible.

Captain Carl Ricchard read the report and said 'Yeah, yeah,' he'd heard it all before.

His job wasn't to question the outcome, only to act as a taxi service and get them to the North Pole, and back in one piece! He had done the trip seven times, three times as first officer, and the last ones as Captain. So, he knew what to expect.

The Fokker friendship F27  Is powered by 2 pit prop engines and, for over 50 years, was probably one of the most versatile and trustworthy planes in the air.  It pretty much, took over from the much loved and admired Dakota DC3. The F27 was designed to fly at nearly all altitudes, and in very trying conditions. It was able to take off and land in very restricted areas.  Not exactly on a postage stamp, but pretty close. A well-chosen plane for this operation.

The plane was kept, ready for action at a moment's notice, in a well-equipped hangar in Murmansk, a small town in Finland. Carl Ricchard would be the Flight Captain. David Hendrix would be first officer. Wally Oomalo a well-qualified assistant first officer. Jenni Hayward would be both, communication officer, and a very experienced meteorologist. Carl was happy with the crew. He knew that in an emergency, any of the flight crew could bring the plane back with great assurance. The other members on board were there for the purely technical reasons of recording the predetermined frozen landmasses.

I have at least five cameras set up to take a range of photographs from differing angles, and, more importantly, the infrared unit capable of emitting invisible sonic waves, and of course, receiving the rays back for further analysis in the laboratory in London.

The history of discovering  useful evidence from previous expeditions had been less than successful over the past few years. Some of them have been extraordinarily interesting and productive. Sadly, the vast majority were a total washout. The one inescapable fact has been that they have become exponentially expensive.

In the post war years, most of the initial expeditions had been carried out using reconnaissance flights, similar to the one currently being considered. It took people of great wisdom and foresight to understand just how much you could learn from the past.

Obviously, they didn't actually expect to locate intact remains of animals, or for that matter, humans, from prior expeditions. Nevertheless, because of the frozen environment, they had discovered various animal carcases which were amazingly intact, to the point that they could assess the gender of the animal and occasionally how it met its demise.

It should be recorded here, that very few carcasses of human beings have ever been discovered. The results of which, are not readily available for publication. Mainly from political interference. Bloody politicians!! But there have been two cases that have provided the scientific world with extremely valuable answers that are always interesting if not spectacular.

For example: the age of the man, the clothing he was wearing, if the contents of the stomach were available, what the chap had for breakfast that perilous morning, his nationality, and, possibly, his ethnicity.

Over the years, those in charge, have explained how relatively easy it is to, pinpoint exactly where the previous expedition had been to; and yet, due to the vagaries of the weather, how incredibly difficult it is to know precisely where they had actually been less than couple of hours ago. As per usual, the weather changed everything! So, for all sorts of reasons, this one was destined to be one of the last of the great expeditions.

Good luck!

# CHAPTER TWO

Stay safe, and try not to come back empty handed.

The old  F 27 rolled out of the Murmansk hangar. It was already fuelled and prepared for action. The cameras were rechecked and correctly in place.  The crew were itching to go. They had to wait for the Captain, who was getting last minute clearance from the civil aviation department.

As he walked across the tarmac, everyone could tell it was good news. Captain Ricchard smiled and gave them the thumbs up sign, as he went through his ultimate outer plane flight check.

He climbed on board and smilingly said, 'Ok folks, let's do it.'

Actually, there isn't a lot to say at this point. The plane duly arrived at the designated Arctic area, and the weather kindly allowed them to crisscross the vast site allowing the technical folk to complete their task with almost monotonous ease.

They were back in Murmansk by late afternoon.
A good job well done!!

Luck had nothing to do with it!

# CHAPTER THREE

What the hell is that?

It was, of course, another six weeks before the results of the expedition were available for assessment. Frankly, checking the screened results is, one of the most boring jobs you can imagine. In very real terms, literally just gazing at seemingly endless expanses of pure white North Pole landscape, with the occasional pale blue thrown in, for good measure.

Somewhat understandably, they could become rather blasé about the monotony of the whole operation.

Oh, for a good blob of something resembling blood red. Or at least, a bit of wholesome gore every now and again. Only joking. They actually took it very seriously, after all that's why they were there. Naturally the senior scientists were deadly serious about their work, but even they got a bit twitchy at times. Equally naturally, the chances of finding anything significant was almost unbackably remote.

Just keep looking!

Jennifer Werner had just started her work day at the laboratory, and was hoping to get back to her boyfriend David, to finish what they had started the previous night, when the damned alarm clock, noisily interrupted their enthusiastic love making. Hate those annoying alarm clocks! Jennifer drove to the laboratory and shouted hello to all her work mates, then sighed as she began her daily routine. Boring, boring, boring.

Another tedious day but, that's why they pay the big bucks, she smilingly reminded herself. Five more hours to go. She went through the routine so often that her one day, blurred into all the previous others. THEN, in the late afternoon. What was that? She checked what she thought she saw, then checked again. Jennifer steeled herself and scanned the computer screen, she looked again, and again. She shook her head and argued with herself. 'I must have made a mistake.'

Her analytical mind overrode her misgivings she said to herself that it can't be but there is something there.

She toyed with the idea of leaving it until tomorrow. But luckily our Jennifer was made of sterner stuff. She phoned the head office with the certain knowledge that, they would definitely expect her to stay whilst her apparent discoveries were checked. She could be here for another two hours. Ah, poor David. Poor me!

The senior analyser arrived very quickly, running all the way to the laboratory. Maybe he had a reason to get back to his home. In his case, almost certainly a televised game of soccer! Jennifer simply said. 'I think this may be of interest.' They both allowed themselves to snap into concentration mode.

Together, they looked at the very dark spot and decided that, yes, there was something, probably a polar bear. They zoomed in, and, for the first time realised that it was something at least significantly dark, and smaller, much smaller, than a polar bear.  Could it be a? They both went through the process of nominating a possible. That's what the discoveries are called until further lengthy investigations were carried out. From now on whatever else happened, it would be out of their hands.

Wow! What started out as a frustratingly predictable day for all of them had become pretty exciting for everyone, especially Jennifer, except David of course, he would have to wait!

# CHAPTER FOUR

There are four possibles, two look really ok, the other two, well!

Obviously the possible would require checking out by a range of experts, and for some reason that process always seemed to take an abundance of time, and they don't have an abundance of that. Again, the rotten weather, spoiled their plans.

The decision of the Society was based on the various expert scientists all being sure of their judgment. They usually tried to present a united front. Unfortunately, it's the team of accountants who made the final decision, and they would frequently present a wishy-washy front.

But the occasional stalemate was successfully overcome by the sheer enthusiasm of the members. The Chairman of the board, Sir Peter Roderick, addressed the committee, 'Gentlemen, a great deal of our precious recourses will be tied up in this venture, and, as you all know. The flight reconnaissance costs, whilst vital, are chicken feed, compared to the land expedition costs.' So many facets had to be considered. Sir Peter enumerated a list, which was obvious to all concerned. A suitable ship would be the first item to be procured. Specialised ice trackers would be needed.

Refrigerated transport, both on sea and land travel.  Absolutely essential, but  most difficult, and expensive of all, is permission from the Greenland government. Never a foregone conclusion. Last of all lots of luck. The most expensive item of all.'

Sir Peter smiled at the assembled scientists, managers and engineers and very simply said, 'However we think this one has legs and, I'm delighted to tell you that the operation is going ahead. I now need to advise you that you have 8 weeks to get prepared,' He smiled as he announced, 'I suppose we are lucky that were dealing  with frozen carcasses. They won't be going anywhere soon!' he chortled. 'Thank you for your time and your patience. Bon voyage! I

will, of course see you prior to your departure.
Good morning gentlemen, please forgive me, and
ladies, where would we be without you.''

CHAPTER FIVE

Look, there it is!

The ship left on the twenty third of January. The weather at the pole should hopefully, be just starting to improve and that made for a quicker and safer voyage. All things being equal, it was worth the wait. The ship arrived at the destination, without any incidents.

It took less than a day to offload the equipment and get the search party organised. Literally, thirty hours later they were on the ice and heading to the first possible, search area.

It doesn't matter how many times you've been on an expedition.  In this environment the unknown is always very exciting, and at times, awesomely terrifying! Their job was to discover the, as yet, unproven photographed area, then try to pinpoint the exact site, and of course, focus on the already established dark spot and, if at all possible, bring back the carcass to England for further analysis.

Sounds easy enough!

Their quest should have been somewhat more precise due to all the knowledge they had prior to leaving home site.

With all that data, you'd think it would be ridiculously simple to hone in to just one poor old dead polar bear who wasn't going anywhere. Life in the science world has never been that easy! They checked the multitudes of cross references, and expected to zoom in to the already nominated, dark spot.

As if to annoy them on purpose, the weather turned very ungallant. They had spent four days in one area with nothing to show for it. Not one sniff of the thing! Whatever it was.

OSSIE TO THE RESCUE-------

Brian Osborne, Ossie, pointed towards the cliff of dark blue ice and communicated electronically with the team leader, and, after gesticulating somewhat overenthusiastically, shouted into the mouthpiece. 'There's something over there,   and it doesn't look anything like as big as a polar bear carcass to me.' Within ten minutes the whole team had arrived at site and all could see what Ossie proudly pointed at.

Sven Harrsen, the team leader, rather pompously said, 'Well ladies and gentlemen, I think we have found something viable. I can't see exactly what it is but, it's bigger than a seal.'

Ossie interrupted and said. 'Well matey it's not a f*****g polar bear. Frankly, I think it looks more like a human being, all hunched up like that.'

The general buzz from the massed party pretty much agree with Ossie. Man or beast, it appeared to be encased in a cocoon of solid ice. The decision was arrived at very quickly, whatever it turned out to be, it must be investigated as soon as possible.

The logical place had been chosen; it was the well-prepared Investigation Laboratory at Farnborough in England. Sven Harrsen contacted Sir Peter Roderick, who listened attentively, and shouted over the line, 'Oh well done, that's splendid, of course, we'll need as much electronic evidence as possible, and anything else you've got for that matter. Our congrats.' to everyone in the party.'

Once the data came through electronically, Peter Roderick and the other directors were equally excited. Even the accountants had the occasional smile on their world-weary faces. The chief accountant commented, rather begrudgingly, 'that's splendid, but whatever you do bring it back in one piece and, in the frozen state it was discovered in.'

F*****g idiot, how else would we bring it back? Yeah right! Sven listened to the experts as they reminded him of the task ahead. It doesn't matter how often you are faced with this sort of problem, it's always a ticklish operation, and every situation is different. There simply isn't a How-To manual for this job.

Fortunately, they were blessed with some very practical souls in the squad and they performed brilliantly. They got on with it, and did it.

Nevertheless, it took them over a day and a half to remove the block of ice and get it safely to the mother ship. Equally  capable of maintaining the mysteriously valuable contents.

So goodbye Iceland and, hello England once more.

# CHAPTER SIX

Buried treasure and then some!

The ship arrived back in England just 18 days after they left. It was now the first of February.

A beaming Sir Peter Roderick was there to meet them. And congratulate them on their achievements. 'If only I was forty years younger,' he said, without a great deal of conviction. None the less, only Sir Peter and the chief accountant were at the dock to welcome them. This was done on purpose due to all the anticipated publicity that discoveries like this tend to create.

The last find of this magnitude caused massive worldwide interest. Later it turned out to be an almost farcical error. Two ill directed seals trying to keep warm as they sadly passed away. This time, best to wait secretly until they are sure of themselves. Then watch out world.

Under exactingly controlled conditions, the specimen was removed from the transport and set up in the laboratory. Sir Peter was thrilled with the find. It was to become even more fascinating as the clinically controlled thawing took place. By now, they were pretty certain that the contents of the ice cube was in fact, a male human being. The clinic had been specifically prepared for just such an operation as this. However, it was well understood that they had almost no data to refer to with regards to the results that the earlier experiments had achieved. Hence it was vital to be utterly, as careful as possible. The whole world was watching.

But those crafty English were frugal about the information they released to the cosmos. Bit by, bit, by juicy bit. Sister Barbra Collins was in charge of caring for and observing the controlled changes as they occurred to the corpse as it was slowly thawing in the laboratory.

The body of the man, they were now sure of the gender, was held in medically controlled conditions. Every organ of his body was being monitored to allow the corpse to come back to ambient temperature as normally as possible. The management team decided that they should keep a film of the man's progress, one way or another.

Naturally a complete medical dossier was also kept, detailing all the many changes that they expected. They were as carefully monitored as one could imagine. The stoic Sister Barbra turned out to be a marvellous choice. Whilst still quite young she turned out to be a remarkably dedicated  medico. Obviously, there were other well experienced staff to observe the body on a 24-hour basis. He would never be left alone. But Barbra was the senior sister. A dedicated woman with years of experience looking after patients and monitoring them as they continued to progress. Of course, this was the quietest one she'd ever known.

The next 48 hours, however, would change her life forever, and pretty much everyone else's.

# CHAPTER SEVEN

A flicker was all it took!

The body of the poor old patient that they had named Boris, had been stripped and covered with a clinical examination gown. The dedicated Sister realised immediately that the boyo wasn't really all that old.   In fact, he would have been quite young, and yes, he was really muscular, and about the same age as her.

Oh yes, and really fit.   A strong physique, good hands. A really rather handsome young man. Ah well! Back to work. She left Boris in the extremely capable hands of the weekend staff. Of course, they knew what they were doing, and they had her mobile number if anything important happened. Barbra blissfully took time off  over the weekend to unwind. She played golf with three other ladies.  The whole point of the game, being to hit an uncaring, ill directional, little white ball into an unforgiving hole.  It infuriated her.

The game is called golf, mainly because all the other fruity four letter words were infuriatingly used up elsewhere. Barbra despised the game with such a passion that she played it single-mindedly, week in, week out. No way would it get the better of her! Stupid s*****g ball.

Three days later she was back in the laboratory, checking that everything was all as it should be. Boris looked pretty much the same. But with the exception that his colour seemed to have altered ever so slightly. Oh really, don't be so ridiculous she smilingly thought to herself as she passed him by.

 She ran back- and stared at Boris for a while. His right eye lid fluttered.

F**k me dead, the bastard's alive!

# CHAPTER EIGHT

Give the man a chance.

All hell broke loose. Within three and a half minutes every doctor, every scientist, every nurse, literally sprinted to the controlled ward. The senior physician very quietly said, 'Excuse me, ladies and gentlemen,' as he made his way into the ward. At least twenty eyes were staring at Boris.

Then… nothing. Absolutely nothing. The silence was deafening.

At least ten minutes went by.

At last Sister Barbra quietly said, 'Look, my God, I'm sure I saw a movement.' The response was immediate and unanimous.

Boris was somehow alive.

But how?  And under what conditions?  Nobody knew his real name, or where he came from. And literally, no one was prepared even to estimate just how long he had been in the hibernated state. Was it 12 months?  Was it 5 years?   Someone suggested he might have been lost during the Second World War.  Oh, come on that's, ridiculous, no one could last that long. Obviously they immediately dismissed the thought and gazed in wonder at Boris.

He in turn, simply stared back at them all, and never once uttered a sound.

It was, somewhat naturally assumed that he didn't speak English, so, at various times people were invited in to chat away in their native tongue in the hope that Boris would react to a friendly language. Frustratingly, absolutely nothing. No reaction. He just stared at them; his expression was one of total bewilderment.

Sister Barbra felt incredible sympathy for Boris, she frequently sat with him and just held his hand and stroked his forehead in a Florence Nightingale sort of way. She sensed that the man was horrifyingly lost. Barbra's natural instincts were to assume responsibility for his wellbeing.

She fed him, made sure that he was clean, and as comfortable as possible. She continued to talk to her unanimatedly silent patient, in a way that she hoped would help him to begin to trust her. Barbra, of course fully realised that, to an outside observer, she looked as though she was talking to herself.

The lovely sister didn't care; she simply smiled radiantly at Boris with the assumption that he understood every word that she spoke. The powers that be had made the wise decision that no television would be allowed in his room, and for that matter, no radio either. The monitoring instruments that he had been attached to were also removed. They caused as much fear as anything to the poor silent man. So, in practical terms, no outside influences would be able to distract him, or cause him any more confusion than he was already in.

His cocoon of ice was replaced with one of controlled silence another two months passed without any obvious progress. It was fair to say that physically he had improved somewhat, but, as his opportunity for exercise was naturally limited to just his immediate surroundings. Even that didn't seem to help particularly. Really, both physically and mentally, he was in a neutral abeyance!

That didn't stop Sister Barbra from being as positive as ever, she enthusiastically chatted to Boris about her life. Her almost obsessional admiration for the works of Edward Elgar, and, of course, John Lennon's really good stuff. Oh yes, and her clumsy struggles with the game of golf.

She even told him what she thought about the inventors of the game, and what they could do with the little white balls, one at a time, and anything else that crossed her mind.  Boris was the perfect audience. Never once did he disagree with her, just stared at her face.

Now and again she thought she saw a flicker of interest, but no, not really!  It must have been her imagination.

# CHAPTER EIGHT

Welcome—welcome—welcome!!

Saturday afternoon. Barbra had given up golf for the time being, and had joined her girlfriends to play cricket for the local team, she was actually a pretty good right-handed opener.  This afternoon was just a training session, but an important one, she was being considered as one of the openers, so she had to be there!

She was still at the clinic and of course dressed in her rather austere nursing uniform. Barbra was finished for the day.  All she had to do was wait for the next nursing shift to show up and she would be off for the long weekend. She smiled and waved to Boris.  And, as she started to leave, she blew him a kiss and said, 'Ok sweetness I'm off to the cricket.' She didn't reach the door but heard the unusual sound.

'Bower, Bower, Bower.'

Barbra stopped dead in her tracks. She ran back and stared at Boris.   His expression had changed to one of, almost panic. Barbra literally whispered, 'Bower?' A long pause. 'Do you mean you are a bowler, are you? Talking about the game of cricket?'

Boris nodded his head and shouted, 'A bower, a bower.' She walked back to him and smiled as she held his hand and kissed his fingers. Not a really emotional girl. But, Wow, Wow, Wow.

She simply stared at him and stroked his brow.

Absolutely nothing was said.

The chief surgeon had followed all this via the observation screen.  He very wisely allowed the two of them to quietly comfort each other.  The doctor knew, that somehow, they had broken through the barrier and possibly this could be the beginning of his return to normality. Cricket would have to wait. Barbra simply put her head on Boris's shoulder and quietly wept. He put his arm around the lovely sister and comforted her.

# CHAPTER NINE

Who do you think you are?

The next few weeks were fraught in almost every way.  Barbra had injured herself by falling over in the shower.  She hurt her right shoulder quite badly but, the main problem was a cut on her thigh.   Her doctor told her that she would need a course of antibiotics, which ruled her out of being in contact with Boris since he was still cocooned in the isolation ward.

Barbra was, of course, very much aware of the medical procedure.  However, it didn't stop her from feeling great compassion for this lonely fellow human being. And in an odd way she sensed that there was empathy between the two of them.

The ensuing three weeks allowed the doctors and specialists to try to bring Boris into the complex world without scaring him half to death. Naturally, they began by talking cricket, which seemed to be a trigger into his past life.  Whatever that might turn out to be.

They chatted to him about all the great international players and even mentioned some of the pre-Second World War greats.

No reaction in any way.

By now they assumed that he was of British decent, mainly because of the cricket interests. They talked about other sports and politics, and naturally the latest in show business news and, well, anything else that they felt might connect with him.

All he did was stare at them.

It was another fourteen days before Barbra was allowed back into the hygienic atmosphere. The doctors understood that Barbra had developed a wonderful knack of talking about ordinary subjects, but still be somewhat probing about well, pretty much anything she could think of.

 She told Boris about the accident which had stopped her going to the cricket.  Boris immediately showed some interest   and stared at Barbra.

She mentioned the meal she cooked last night.   It was beef vindaloo curry and rice with cucumber and mint sauce. Delicious.

'Would you like to try some, frankly it's a bit hot, but very tasty. What's your favourite curry?'

Not a word did he utter.

What was he thinking? Was he thinking at all?

The medical fraternity, along with main experts in the psychiatric field, felt a great sympathy for the poor fellow.   But they realised that breaking into his trapped mind was probably going to take a very long time to unravel.

The obvious relations that Sister Barbra had developed with her patient was simply essential. It was almost a month later that they got a further breakthrough. The predictable routine in the morning meant that he got breakfast drearily at the same time, that is eight o'clock on the dot.

Barbra set the tray in front of Boris, this morning it was, 'Umm, scrambled eggs on toast with some fresh fruit.'

Barbra smilingly chattered, as she walked away 'There you are my lovely.'  Boris replied without hesitation.  'Oh that looks nice.'

Barbra quickly responded. 'Well sir I hope it's to your liking,' she sprinted back to the bed side.

'What did you say?'

 He just smiled at her and kept eating his scrambled eggs on toast, with a cup of tea, milk, with no sugar! Very pleasant!

Barbra, with furrowed brow, tried to sound as casual as she could, so, asked again. 'Did you say you thought it was what?'

Boris just smiled and said, 'nice.'

It should be understood that literally any sign of improvement was gladly accepted. But sometimes, analysed by the experts, to the point of missing the blatantly obvious.

Barbra was always invited to the progress meetings, they recognised just how vital her special friendship had become to his recovery. They all said that, in simple terms, it was going to take months or, maybe even years to make a breakthrough. They had to be patient with their patient!

## CHAPTER TEN

What age are you??

They were very careful about the questions put to him. The last thing they wanted to do was shock the poor guy into clamming up even more than he presently was. Make it precise, but keep it light. But not our Barbra, she was developing a genuine fondness for Boris, so she just nattered away about anything she could think of. His improvement was all she cared about. And it didn't really matter how long it took. Barbra had become used to Boris's simple answers to her questions. Occasionally, proffering basic sentences that were quite encouraging.

One Friday morning, Barbra was sitting on the bed end filling in her report when…

'How is our beloved Queen?' Boris asked in such a natural way that the slightly bemused Barbra had to regain her composure before she answered in a conversational way. 'Oh well, from what I know she's particularly fit for a woman who's now a great grandmother, as you probably know she'll be ninety-three years old on her next birthday, that'll be cause for a bit of a knees up wont it?'

Boris just stared at her for a long time then said. 'Don't be ridiculous. The woman can't be more than forty years old.' Somewhat shocked, Barbra tried to think of all the European royal courts that could promote such a retort. None came to mind.

Barbra stood up and casually moved herself to the end of the bed. After a long, rather convoluted minute and a half, she asked the obvious question. 'Which, um, Queen are you talking about?'

Boris smiled at Barbra and replied. 'Well obviously our beloved Queen Victoria.' Barbra, stared at Boris, and then stared again, whilst she tried to adjust the confusion in her befogged brain. Not easy, not easy at all.

She could hear the stampede of medical feet as they sprinted down the hall, every one of the doctors and physicians trying to look casual, as they tumbled into the room and stared at the very relaxed Boris. The smiling masks betrayed the expressions on their well-trained confused faces.

In point of fact, none of them had the faintest idea what to ask of the poor man. Mainly because the anticipated answers all sounded so bizarrely unbelievable.

Doctor Nimrod Savoury, the chief physician smilingly said. 'I hope you'll excuse us for just a few moments, couple of things we need to address, right, ok, right, ladies and gentlemen, if you will.' The august body of doctors immediately went into a sort of rugby huddle outside the ward.

One of the situations they all agreed upon, was the need to be very careful about disturbing Boris's recent improvement. All the staff conceded that, and chorused, 'Well, yes naturally, yes, obviously. He couldn't possibly have been alive during the reign of QV.' They nodded. 'I mean, that would be ridiculous, his mind must have been addled in some way,' Doctor Savoury said.

Whilst they wholeheartedly agreed with him, none of them came up with a plausible reason for Boris's comment.

Sister Barbra joined them in the meeting outside the ward and listened very attentively, then wisely cautioned.  'I believe I have the man's trust and, with your blessing, I'll broach the questions that need to be asked. I must tell you, I'm certain that he must be confused by this very action from us right at this moment.  He is by no means a stupid man, just a lost soul. Anyway, you'll be able to monitor our conversation via your George Orwell screen, won't you?'

Barbra left the meeting and returned to the ward. Deep down, she was as conflicted as anyone could be. How could a man who looks as young as Boris possibly have any knowledge of a queen who died over a hundred and twenty years ago? It didn't make any sense.

She decided to write down options that could account for it:

1. Was he a history student?

2. Was his family ever involved with the royal household?

3. Did he own some valuable mementos from the Victorian era?

4. Did Victoria ever open the batting England? No that's silly, she was a spin bowler. Ha Ha!

Barbra mentally cajoled herself. 'Oh don't be so idiotic, get a grip on yourself girl. Ok, let's start with the obvious ones.' She smiled at Boris and told him as honestly as she could that she wanted to help him to find his background and fill in the confusing gaps.

She started.

'We call you Boris but, is that you real name?' Boris laughed and said. 'No of course not, it's Sebastian Hadley. When you called me Boris, well, I didn't really know who you were talking about. I thought it was a joke.'

Barbra said, 'No, not really a joke, but this information is much better, at last we are getting close to you. Can you tell me where you were born?'

The reply came quickly and fluently, 'In a little village called Chipping Norton, it's in the Midlands, and I miss it very much. It seems like quite a few years since I've been there.'

Barbra told him that she knew the area quite well and added, 'Oh this is marvellous, we are starting to get to know you at last. Could you remind us of your birthday, we aren't entirely sure of it?'

'Of course, I'll tell you, I might get a nice cake out of it. It's the fourteenth of June, so you see I'm a contented little Gemini,' said the now known as, Sebastian with a laugh in his voice.'

Barbra had silly smile on her face as she asked the blindingly obvious question. 'And um, er, er, what exact year was that?'

'Oh, that's a good'un, its fourteenth of June, 1811 ...year of our Lord.' Sebastian smiled proudly as he tried to remember the last time anyone asked his birthday, it seemed a long time ago, a very long time ago. He couldn't quite recall who it was that asked the question.

# CHAPTER ELEVEN

The truth, and nothing but the truth.

It's almost impossible to imagine the noise of various feet thundering down the hall like a rugby scrum. The scientific staff, all presumed to be a serious group of folks. They got to the vacuum operated doors of the ward and unanimously stopped to regain whatever composure they once had.

By the time they entered the ward, they had adopted a serious expression on their collectively august faces. Barbra had a bemused look on hers. The only one who looked anything like normal was Sebastian. He cast his eyes over the assembled throng and simply asked, 'Anything wrong?' The chorus of voices trumpeted back. 'No, no, no, of course not, we were just discussing how to celebrate your birthday and, er, we have got a few surprises for you.'

Barbra had the most incredulous expression on her face but she at least smiled at Sebastian and exclaimed the most understated sentence in her life! Barbra whispered to Sebastian. 'We have things to tell you that I believe will shock you. Firstly, did you ever think about the instruments you were connected to, when you first arrived here?'

Sebastian's smile disappeared and he gave a confused shake of the head. She explained, 'They were all technical gauges which allowed us to monitor your progress.' She held his hand as the words tumbled out. 'Secondly, there's no easy way to say this except, we, none of us really know how it happened but, you appear to have been in a coma for, well we don't know how long, but we believe you have slept through most of the nineteenth century and all of the twentieth century. And now the biggest shock of all. Sebastian this is the year twenty sixteen. We believe that you have been in suspended animation for nearly one hundred and seventy years, your body protected by the frozen environment.'

Sebastian in profound shock nodded his head and whispered, 'I suppose that all my family are dead and buried.'

Barbra held his hand as she solemnly nodded. 'That's one of the things we should be able to help you with. Sebastian there are so many more shocks that you have to face over the next few weeks. We have to tell you that the world has changed dramatically. With your permission, we want to bring in, what we refer to as a television set. If you can possibly imagine, it's something like a magic lantern, only much, much more so. The one thing I want you to realise is that, we all care about you a lot and know that the next month or so, is going to be the hardest you have ever faced.' She clung onto Sebastian's hand and smiled as much as she could. 'Is there anything you want to ask me or any other of the doctors and scientists? We will do our very best to answer your questions, with as much honesty as we possibly can.'

The assembled throng of medicos all nodded enthusiastically, without really having the faintest idea where to start. Sebastian closed his eyes, and disappeared into a cloak of confusion.

## CHAPTER TWELVE

The past, versus the future.

Barbra made the decision to, literally put her life on hold for the next few months.

The clinic, very wisely put a bed/ sitting room  at her disposal. So, she could be with him, day and night, if necessary. Golf, cricket, social life, it would all have to wait in line. Sebastian first, that's it.

They were able to check the records and discovered that an expedition had actually gone to the North Arctic at round about that time. Nothing had been reported about the outcome of the trek and that they were never heard of again. Communications at that time were almost nil, so they were forced to presume that Sebastian had unbelievably survived the appalling conditions and was now the ultimate survivor.

The knowledge was so devastating they decided to keep it to themselves. If Sebastian ever posed the question to them, it was certain that they would answer as honestly as possible.

From that moment on, Barbra shared her life with Sebastian, ate all her meals with him, and made sure to be with him when the momentous things happened. Like the first time he saw a television set, for instance. It was collectively decided that a TV could be introduced to Sebastian, mainly because they could monitor the programmes, and always have someone with him to try to explain exactly what was going on. No easy task, Sebastian wanted to know everything.

Primarily they made the decision to introduce him to a soccer match, because, well, like cricket  and soccer, he seemed to love sport, and understood it, so it was, hopefully, something he could relate to.  It was hoped that it just might prove to be a sort of psychological hook to get him to ask questions. Any questions.

They chose a soccer match between Manchester United and Wolverhampton Wanderers. A good match, so they could talk about that with some knowledge. So long as he didn't ask them to interpret the off-side rule. Even God couldn't fathom that one out!

Incidentally, Man U, won, three nil.

The TV was brought into the room and set up, and of course switched on via the remote control. Sebastian gave a little gasp as the picture came into view

# CHAPTER THIRTEEN

The start of a new journey.

The next three months were both extraordinary and disturbing.  Sebastian turned out to be the most amazingly open-minded character. He, somehow accepted   most of the visions he saw on TV, but literally questioned almost everything else he saw but didn't understand.

The TV was a source of endless fascination, he looked behind it, and stroked it, and found absolute fascination with the remote control unit, and was particularly amused with the volume control, quiet---- loud--- ear shatteringly loud. He  giggled  at  all  of  them. There was never a time when he didn't have a group of people with him, all of them capable of explaining what was going on, via the TV. Dr Savoury and the psychiatrists were as engrossed with Sebastian, as he was with the TV programmes.  Oddly enough, they began  to look at the TV through his eyes.

Sebastian felt great concern for the soccer players who disappeared off to the side of the screen, he anxiously asked what had happened to them. If they had been injured in any way! Whilst the Savoury team understood exactly where they had gone, they began to realise how much we take utterly for granted.

## A BREATH OF FRESH AIR

They soon realised that his questions came from a deeply probing mind, and they should enrich his thoughts with more complex viewing. He was introduced to the BBC News programmes. He, all too soon, discovered some of the horrors of the world we all live in. He was as shocked as we all should be. There was no doubt that the time had come for his first venture into the outside world. A big step for everyone. None more so than for Sebastian.

The medical fraternity understood exactly how vulnerable he would be to the outside World. At least he was fit, strong, and itching to venture into the world outside so.

Off we go!!!

Barbra drove a nifty little foreign car. She offered to be his chauffer and take him around the immediate area. A splendid thought, she was an excellent driver and her car was everything it should be. Sebastian had, by now, seen a number of cars driving on the TV set. Naturally, he hadn't the faintest idea what they actually did, but he figured, well, there are quite a few of them. Gosh, maybe a hundred, or more!

<h1 style="text-align:center">CHAPTER FOURTEEN</h1>

Nearly six months after Sebastian had arrived back in Britain, he took his first step into the new and, for him, challenging world. He was unquestionably an optimist of the highest degree and, it seemed, as though his basic honesty had affected most of the doctors and the nursing staff that had looked after him.

But none, literally none, had come anywhere near the affection he felt for Barbra. More than just her medical nursing, which was everything it should be, she smoothed the path into the present, and for him, a terrifying world. She found a way to diminish the fear and surrounded him with the love of another human.

Monday morning. After an excellent breakfast of sausages and tomatoes on toast, with tea, milk and no sugar, of course, Barbra casually mentioned to Sebastian that she was going for a drive. Not very far, just into town and back again. 'Would you like to join me, it won't take much more than an hour,' she tried to make it as casual as she could. Sebastian thought about it for just slightly over a second and said. 'Oh alright, what should I wear?' The weather was smiling on them and it was quite warm for that time of year. Sebastian put on his, by now, well-worn athletic suit. Excellent choice

Amazingly enough Barbra was a lot more nervous than he was. For the first time since, well a long time, he walked outside and smelled the fresh air. Good, really good. This was not a man to timidly peep around corners. He strode out. Barbra had gone ahead and slowly brought her car to the entrance hall that contained our Sebastian, all agog with anticipation.   He walked over to the car and smiled at Barbra.

'So, this is the car, I suppose there are quite a few of them,' Barbra just smiled and nodded, 'Oh yes, quite a few.' He didn't ask one question, just stroked it, smelt it, looked all over it including underneath it. 'Ah ha, so it's an automobile, very nice.' Barbra opened the door for him and he immediately got in.

The only thing she said was. 'Do up the seat belt please,' she showed him how to do it. He started to laugh, the car was immobile and he had to put this ridiculous belt thing on. Of course, he did as he was told and said, 'Now what?' Barbra, a fine little driver, took a deep breath as she let the clutch out slowly, and off they went.

His first trip in a thing called a car. Gosh!

Sebastian hardly asked any questions at all. He was utterly bemused at the sheer brilliance of the noisy thing. Farnborough, being the place it was designed to be, that is, one of the major test areas for aeroplanes of all types, but mainly jets, had many planes on the ground.

Less than four minutes later a small  jet-propelled plane thundered over the airport before approaching the landing strip. Sebastian was both scared of the incredible noise and vibrations it created.   How could anything that small make that amount of noise? It's a massive understatement, to say that his whole world had been turned upside-down by the time he got back to the hospital

Then the questions came. Barbra happily allowed the assembled crew to try to answer his myriad thoughts. Quite frankly his memory proved to be excellent, he was asking about things that we all take for granted. For example why did the car stop when you pressed a little lever thing on the floor? How on earth could you drive around and not hit all those other cars. There's no easy answer to that! And no one wanted to take on electricity. An almost impossible subject to explain to a person who has never seen it before. They gave up after trying to explain the concept of an electric tooth brush. It doesn't make logical sense.

The most asked questions being, what does electricity look like? And if you turn a switch on, where does the electricity go when you turn it off? But his unanswerable questions were always ones of innocent intelligence. After watching a news report about the Middle East, he wanted to know why we couldn't see how all the fighting couldn't possibly bring people together.

No one even tried to answer that.

# CHAPTER FIFTEEN

Still the important things were about to happen.

It was the glorious season of cricket. Where no man ever said at bad word about another man in cream trousers. Of course not chaps!

Barbra swanned into Sebastian's room to say ta ta, she was off to the cricket. Sebastian stared at her then asked. 'Do you mean that you're going to watch your father, or your brother, or even,' a pause, 'a boyfriend play?' Barbra simply said, 'Of course not, I'm playing for my local team, I open the batting.'

Sebastian looked at her, and not for the first time said, 'Don't be ridiculous, women don't play cricket anyway you might get hurt. It's a man's game.' Barbra was going to tell him a few home truths about the modern roles of men and women but decided against it. 'Humph!' was all she said as she left his room. Without further ado, and, moving along to Monday morning---

At approximately eight fifteen, Barbra brought Sebastian his breakfast tray.   Plonked it down, unceremoniously, in front of him.   Almost threw the local paper to him and simply said. 'Back page, cricket column. Look who scored forty-three not out,' she started to walk away with an expression on her face that could put world peace back twenty years, but came back and, less than graciously, said, 'and I took two catches in the slips.' She marched womanfully away.

Poor old Sebastian, so much to learn, so little time.  But gosh--what a teacher.

It was becoming obvious to those in the know, that Barbra and Sebastian had found a quasi-romantic attachment to each other. Neither of them had made a move in that direction. Why? There's no easy answer to that, however, it was just a matter of time.

Oh, that overworked cliché. But well. That's Sebastian for you; he would probably meander through life, and only regret missed opportunities, after the band had finished playing!

Not, however, our Barbra in any way, she found his innocence charming, and his capacity to ask innocuous questions endearing, but she recognised that she would have to do most of the chasing.

Well that's ok, she knew just about everything there was to know about the man, including that he was born two hundred years ago.  That took a bit of digesting. Barbra was made of sterner stuff!

The end of the British summer was beckoning to all and sundry, and with it, the concluding warm weather for another year. And tragically, having to say goodbye to cricket for another season. But hooray for the soccer! Sebastian had talked to a number of his, by now, new friends about Chipping Norton and his past life. Whilst he was entirely certain that the chances of contacting anyone in the village who might have known of his family, or at least their descendants, was virtually impossible. He felt the emotional need to complete his journey and visit the place of his birth, however  heart wrenching may prove to be. Barbra offered to take Sebastian on a trip to his home village.    Very obviously, it was with the blessing  of the medical staff at Farnborough. The consensus being that he, eventually had to face the real world.

Sebastian was making excellent progress in every way, and of course Barbra would be with him on his journey, so yes, the trip was considered a splendid idea, one that would help him to tackle this complex world we live in.

Saturday morning dawned, still quite warm and sunny, hopefully for a few more days yet. An excellent time to go hunting for the past, whilst accompanied with the future.

# CHAPTER SIXTEEN

It took about an hour and a half to get to Chipping Norton.  The traffic on the road was very steady and nothing really happened on the trip.  In the last few months Sebastian had started talking almost nonstop.  Barbara simply believed that he was making up for lost time and eventually he would run out of things to chat about. Most of his nattering was made up of questions, many of them unanswerable by Barbra. She had developed a way of getting Sebastian to remember the point by saying. 'That's a good one, why don't you ask Dr Savoury about it?' that seemed to satisfy his curiosity.

This trip turned out to be totally different. They reached the tiny township of Stow-on- the-Wold. As Sebastian saw the sign post he immediately clammed up.  Barbra understood that Sebastian recognised the place from his past. His whole character  changed very dramatically.

Barbra pulled over to the side of the road. She didn't say a word, just lent across and kissed Sebastian on the cheek, and held his hand for a minute. All she said was, 'it's ok, do you want to continue?' He just nodded.

They quietly drove into Chipping Norton, apart from being bigger, it hadn't changed that much. They drove to the cricket ground and parked the car next to the entrance. It now boasted a new pavilion which was pretty swishy, actually it was built in nineteen forty-seven as part of the post war effort to get the place going. Sebastian was as bemused as everyone believed he would be when he was confronted with the memories of his past. After getting out of the car he immediately held Barbra's hand tightly, too tightly, she completely understood.

Without saying a word, they walked over to the Bell Inn, from the outside it hadn't changed a bit, they walked into the snug bar. It was busy with Saturday trade!

The hotel was inhabited with the local cricket team getting ready to play the last game of the season, their opponents would be the Stratford Wasps. Apparently, a fine team, and one that would challenge all their resources. Sebastian and Barbra listened to all the general hubbub; it was pretty obvious that they were going to have to face a formidable team. Sebastian smiled at Barbra and whispered, 'Nothing's changed.' Barbra, with a fair amount of knowledge said. 'Well I hope they field first, that pitch will take spin.'

Sebastian, stared at Barbra with a new respect for his lovely companion, just nodded and agreed entirely with the cricket - wise authority. She looked around and said. 'Ok boyo I'm going to do some shopping and get the garage to have a look at the clutch, I'll be about an hour, you'll be ok won't you?' Sebastian just smiled and said 'I'm old enough to look after myself, take your time. I'm not going anywhere.' Barbra grinned and blew him a kiss as she left.

There are lots of coincidences in life, this was just one more! Harry Garret the main opening batsman for Chipping Norton, earlier ran over to his car, opened the door and slammed it shut. It really would have been a better idea to have taken his left finger out of it first. Well he didn't, and in a lot of pain he swore, 'F**k me that hurt!' He phoned the Bell Inn pub and explained to the captain that he couldn't play cricket for at least a week. The captain, a man of stoic capacity said quietly, 'Ok vicar we'll try and make do without you, hope you're better soon.'

He turned to the guys in the pub and gave them the tragic news that Harry's finger was all buggered up. Whilst not a traditional medical, or cricket term, it summed the situation up perfectly.

The captain turned to the assembled team and said, 'Well guys we are in trouble, if we can't find an opener, we may have to call it off. Sebastian on the spur of the moment, having heard the drama, and grabbed his chance saying. 'Well I played a bit of cricket in the past.' It must be mentioned that he looked like a cricketer, whatever that means. Except he wasn't wearing creams. So what, they were desperate.

Literally half an hour later he was walking out to the centre pitch to take his stance. 'Middle and off please ump.' With bat in hand he twirled it once, then settled down to face his first ball in a long time. Barbra wasn't there to see him, and that was sad but, c'est la vie.   You can't have everything.

This is really just a tiny coincidence, but it deserves airing so---

You see, Barbra's car needed a bit more attention than anticipated, in fact it took over three hours before it was drivable, and hence she missed the twenty over game completely. No matter everyone seemed happy. In particular Sebastian, who had never heard of a cricket game called twenty /twenty. A bit odd but fairly satisfying.

He said goodbye to his new friends and mentioned that he hoped he would see them next season.   As they drove away Barbra asked Sebastian how the game finished.   Sebastian was oddly very quiet.

'We were lucky, we won by twenty-one runs.' A pause, 'Oh that's good, and how did you go?'  A long pause, Sebastian spoke quietly. 'I got thirty-two runs.'

'Well that's not bad at all.'

It was half way to Stow- on- the- Wold before Barbra  persevered. 'How did you get out?'

'Bowled.' squirmed Sebastian. 'Oh, come on everyone gets out sooner or later, who got your wicket?' Barbra insisted.  The longest pause of all. 'A bowler called E. Smith.' Barbra asked, 'is that Eddie or Ted Smith.'

'No, it was Elizabeth Smith.'

A smile crept over Barbra's face as she looked at Sebastian who eventually had an equally silly smile on his face

Welcome to the truly new world!

# Other books by the author:

**Short Stories**:

Please…Don't Explain
Hold Your Brother
The Honourable Lie
In the Shadow of the Truth
In the Shadow of the Truth and Other Short
Stories

**Plays:**

The Lady in Suite 57
Two for the Price of One
49 Not Out

All print editions of the books available from all
online book stores or directly from the publisher
info.felixpublishing@gmail.com

Books are also available in Kindle format by
downloading the free Kindle App onto any
electronic device on any platform.

# About the Author

Jeremy John Lowley was born during the Second World War in a small town called Urmston, a suburb of Manchester in Lancashire. To the eternal annoyance of his uncle, who was a fanatical cricket fan, in those days you had to be born in Yorkshire to play for the county—Jeremy was never that good anyway!

The family eventually migrated to Cheltenham spa in the Cotswolds a remarkably lovely place, dedicated to the arts and music, Jeremy was lucky to be part of a loving family that encouraged interests in theatre, both drama and musicals.

His education began in Cheltenham where he became interested in engineering eventually becoming a design engineer with a large aeronautical company. He then decided to migrate to Australia, mainly because of the weather, and also that they spoke a sort of English.

Whilst in Western Australia he was offered the chance to read the news on the local ABC radio, this was during the time when the iron ore industries were becoming so important, it would appear that just about every week plane loads of Japanese business men were visiting WA. All of them with virtually unpronounceable names, he was told by various friends that a major war was averted by his ignorance, ah well!

Jeremy was able to continue his love of live theatre and, whilst in Sydney was offered the part of the king in the musical The King and I. It took the talents of a variety of make-up artists to convert his very European face to one that was even vaguely Asian.

He was also lucky to play Malvolio in Twelfth Night and various other parts in classical theatre but maintained a love of comedy.